Bottom-Tier
CHARACTER
TOMOZAKI
Lv.4
YUKI YAKU
Illustration by
Fly

Erika
Konno's
group

TODAY'S
DATE
( )
Aoi
Hinami's
group

The sports tournament begins.

"Well, what's your answer?"
Nakamura was as cool and blunt as ever.

"Um..."

Bottom-Tier Character Tomozaki, Level 4

CONTENTS

1 When your regular attacks improve, adventures get way easier P.1

2 The best games make reconnaissance fun P.33

3 After a difficult quest, your latent abilities rise to the surface P.71

4 Even seemingly unbeatable bosses have weak points P.115

5 Sometimes you'll trigger a flag you've been ignoring when you least expect it P.143

6 A happy ending doesn't mean this game is over P.163

Tsugumi Narita

NARITA

Design Yuko Mucadeya + Caiko Monma (musicagographics)

Bottom-Tier
CHARACTER
TOMOZAKI
Lv.4
Yuki Yaku
Illustration by Fly
YEN ON
New York

Bottom-Tier Character TOMOZAKI Lv.4

YUKI YAKU

Cover art by Fly
Translation by Winifred Bird

JAKU CHARA TOMOZAKI-KUN LV.4
by Yuki YAKU

Original Japanese edition published by SHOGAKUKAN.
English translation rights in the United States of America, Canada, the United Kingdom, Ireland, Australia, and New Zealand arranged with SHOGAKUKAN through Tuttle-Mori Agency, Inc.

Yen On
150 West 30th Street, 19th Floor
New York, NY 10001

Visit us at yenpress.com
facebook.com/yenpress
twitter.com/yenpress
yenpress.tumblr.com
instagram.com/yenpress

First Yen On Edition: August 2020

Yen On is an imprint of Yen Press, LLC.
The Yen On name and logo are trademarks of Yen Press, LLC.

Library of Congress Cataloging-in-Publication Data
Names: Yaku, Yuki, author. | Fly, 1963- illustrator. | Bird, Winifred, translator.
Title: Bottom-tier character Tomozaki / Yuki Yaku ; illustration by Fly ; translation by Winifred Bird.
Other titles: Jyakukyara Tomozaki-kun. English
Description: First Yen On edition. | New York : Yen On, 2019-
Identifiers: LCCN 2019017466 | ISBN 9781975358259 (v. 1 : pbk.) | ISBN 9781975384586 (v. 2 : pbk.) |
ISBN 9781975384593 (v. 3 : pbk.) | ISBN 9781975384609 (v. 4 : pbk.)
Subjects: LCSH: Video games—Fiction. | Video gamers—Fiction.
Classification: LCC PL877.5.A35 J9313 2019 | DDC 895.63/6–dc23
LC record available at https://lccn.loc.gov/2019017466

ISBNs: 978-1-9753-8460-9 (paperback)
978-1-9753-8643-6 (ebook)

10 9 8 7 6 5 4 3 2 1

LSC-C

Printed in the United States of America

Bottom-Tier Character Tomozaki

Lv.4

Characters

Fumiya Tomozaki
Second-year high school student. Bottom-tier.

Aoi Hinami
Second-year high school student. Perfect heroine of the school.

Minami Nanami
Second-year high school student. Class clown.

Hanabi Natsubayashi
Second-year high school student. Small.

Yuzu Izumi
Second-year high school student. Hot.

Fuka Kikuchi
Second-year high school student. Bookworm.

Takahiro Mizusawa
Second-year high school student. Wants to be a beautician.

Shuji Nakamura
Second-year high school student. Class boss.

Takei
Second-year high school student. Built.

Tsugumi Narita
First-year high school student. Easygoing.

Erika Konno
Second-year high school student. Queen of the class.

Common Honorifics

In order to preserve the authenticity of the Japanese setting of this book, we have chosen to retain the honorifics used in the original language to express the relationships between characters.

No honorific: Indicates familiarity or closeness; if used without permission or reason, addressing someone in this manner would constitute an insult.

-san: The Japanese equivalent of Mr./Mrs./Miss. If a situation calls for politeness, this is the fail-safe honorific.

-kun: Used most often when referring to boys, this indicates affection or familiarity. Occasionally used by older men among their peers, but it may also be used by anyone referring to a person of lower standing.

-chan: An affectionate honorific indicating familiarity used mostly in reference to girls; also used in reference to cute persons or animals of either gender.

-senpai: An honorific indicating respect for a senior member of an organization. Often used by younger students with their upperclassmen at school.

-sensei: An honorific indicating respect for a master of some field of study. Perhaps most commonly known as the form of address for teachers in school.

1

When your regular attacks improve, adventures get way easier

The end of summer vacation didn't mean the end of summer, and the heat was stubbornly hanging on into September 1.

I was in a slightly aged classroom, yawning after the first early morning in ages. Across from me was Hinami, sitting up straight with her big eyes open wide and alert.

For the first time in a little over a month, Hinami and I were having a morning meeting in Sewing Room #2.

"All right. Before we talk about the next steps, we need to go over a few things." Hinami sounded as brisk and efficient as always.

"Such as?"

I looked around the classroom. The place didn't feel as run-down as before—maybe because every time we met here, we brushed aside some of the dust and moved the desks and chairs around so it was easier to talk. Now it had a faintly lived-in feeling. What hadn't changed was Hinami's cool attitude.

"You finished training for your part-time job over summer vacation, didn't you? How did that go?" Hinami tucked her silky hair behind one ear as she spoke as clearly and fluidly as ever.

"Oh, that's what you meant… Well, training was two hours a day for five days with the boss and other employees. Nothing special to report. I had a close call with Mizusawa, but I haven't had a chance to talk about it with him yet."

"Gotcha. So nothing's changed since we last talked… In that case, we'd better set your new goals for the second semester today."

"'Kay."

So it was time for more "goals."

We were back to our usual routine after a summer vacation full of challenges: the overnight trip to get Nakamura and Izumi together, my dates with Kikuchi-san, and the argument and reconciliation between Hinami and me. Just like before, Hinami was focused single-mindedly on the future.

"After five full days of training, I was hoping you'd have taken the initiative on some independent study…but I guess I expected too much."

"I know, I know. I'm sorry. I did have good intentions, but…"

"Hmph. Did you wear yourself out rebelling against me?"

"Uh…"

"You're such an open book."

"Shut up, you don't have to tell me."

This was so familiar, interjecting pointless banter into our strategizing for my personal growth.

But…

"Whatever. Anyway, let's talk about your goals moving forward."

"Okay."

There was just one thing.

"We had a minor checkpoint of you going out alone with a girl other than me, and you've completed that objective. So I suppose the next one should be sharing secrets with a girl."

Hinami shifted her gaze away, slightly uncomfortable. Yes, just one small thing had changed.

"…Do you have a problem with that?" she curtly asked.

She was getting my approval for the goals she set.

"No…," I said, reflecting for a moment. "I'm not making any shallow speeches or telling a girl I like her, but otherwise, I'm fine. What did you have in mind?"

I was getting better at comparing Hinami's objectives with my own values and telling her what I thought. She gaped slightly, momentarily surprised by my outspoken reply, but quickly regained her composure.

"What I said, pretty much. When you share a secret with someone, it shows that both of you see the other as special, and it's also a sign of trust.

It'll be a big step toward your mid-term goal, which is to have a girlfriend by the time you start your third year of high school."

"Er, okay."

"But it has to be *mutual.* It's not enough to tell a secret without hearing one or to hear a secret without telling one. You each need to open your hearts to the other."

I'd already thought of Kikuchi-san's secret about writing a novel, but apparently, that wouldn't count because it wasn't mutual. But if I told Kikuchi-san a secret, would that check the box?

As I was thinking, Hinami batted her eyes at me oh-so-vulnerably.

"Just like this secret relationship between you and me…"

"Hey, wha…?"

My face was on fire after her sneak attack. She smiled playfully and watched my reaction.

"What's the matter?"

She peered into my face with her big eyes, delivering the follow-up punch.

"N-nothing…"

"Really?"

She grinned with satisfaction, seeing me so tongue-tied, then resumed her neutral expression and pointed at me.

"You need to strengthen your defenses against this kind of thing. Normie girls are naturally good at getting close to guys. If you can't stand your ground, they'll get the upper hand."

"You…"

As usual, she had me wrapped around her finger, and I pulled myself together. Ugh, shit. My defenses were currently around zero, so this stuff stung. *I will not give in.*

"And I know this is obvious, but I want you to give your daily goals everything you've got. Of course, you can't forget your short- and mid-term goals, either. And finally, the most important thing is—"

"I know!" I interrupted her rapid-fire stream of orders (partially as a retort to her previous jab, too). "If I come across a situation I think would net me some EXP, you want me to take the initiative and jump in."

Hinami blinked twice. "…You got it. Glad you understand."

"Okay."

I raised one eyebrow to show I did. Not long ago, I didn't even know how to make that expression. It was a tiny taste of revenge. She pursed her lips in a brief pout, then quickly grinned.

"The sooner you learn how to improve yourself, the faster things will proceed."

I knew I didn't fully understand her, but even if I couldn't explain why, she made sense.

"That could be." I nodded, feeling oddly satisfied.

"'Cause it *is*."

Hinami looked pleased with my response. Watching her, I had a sneaking suspicion that she had me in the palm of her hand. Well, she *did*. Let's be real.

She was still way beyond my level. All the same, I didn't like constantly losing to her, and I wanted my revenge, so I decided to deliver one more shot.

"Plus, when I figure out my own strats…it's more *fun*."

She furrowed her brows suspiciously. "More fun, huh?"

Hinami examined me up and down, her gaze rising from the tips of my toes all the way up to my head.

"Yeah," I said with an extra shot of confidence. "Priorities, y'know?"

I grinned.

After we'd argued on the platform, we'd had another talk at the place where we first met, and I gave it to her straight. The most important standard for all this was my own desires—what I wanted.

For me, being true to myself was like becoming my character in a game—really throwing myself into something I love and enjoying it to the fullest. *What I wanted* wasn't a temporary misconception or something I had to convince myself to believe. It was real.

Of course, I had no proof for my theory. I couldn't lay it all out with logic. But I'd really pressed this point, and I'd need something to show for it if I wanted Hinami to be convinced. Not that I had any idea when that would happen.

As I thought about all this, the confidence steadily drained from my smile. I was starting to worry, actually, and my smile started feeling like a mask that was covering up my anxiety. *Yeah, what* am *I going to do about all this?*

Hinami must have sussed out my weakness, because she gave me a sadistic look.

"Proving it is certainly going to be a merciless, virtually impossible assignment. I'm looking forward to seeing what you come up with," she said.

"Uh-huh..."

All I could do was nod helplessly as she reminded me that she still had the upper hand. That was the Hinami I knew—she never left herself open for a millisecond, and she refused to let me hide behind ambiguity.

"Anyway, we'll put that aside for now," she said, changing the subject.

"Okay," I agreed. "On to today's assignment?"

She sighed, smiling. "Yes. I'd like you to observe our class for a while."

"What should I observe?"

"For your previous assignments, you've been working on basic skills, such as your expression and way of speaking, and learning the fundamentals for manipulating the mood of a group. You've also completed some basic training on how to establish yourself in a hierarchy."

"Yeah."

I'd made a habit of training my muscles for my expression and posture. I'd practiced getting people to take my suggestions when I went shopping for Nakamura's birthday present and applied that experience during Mimimi's student council speech. I'd joked around with Mizusawa and Nakamura as part of my practice in casual conversation, too. When I thought about it, I'd actually accomplished a lot.

"Which means the next thing you need to do is start applying them."

"Okay." Made sense. "And...you're saying observation is necessary in order to do that?"

Hinami nodded.

"You've built up your abilities and learned the basic rules, and those make up the foundation of some of the skills you've practiced now. You already have most of the basic techniques down, more or less."

"I do?"

"Well, you're not great at them yet, but yes," Hinami said. "Anyway, you don't go and learn new things right after you start applying the basics, do you? Application is just polishing those skills and using them in real situations. This practice is part of polishing, plus you'll develop your ability to decide what to use when. Those two points will be very important… But I don't have to tell you that, right?"

"Yeah…," I said, thinking about *Atafami*. "I get what you're trying to say."

Atafami was the same. Once you learned the basic moves, you had to get better at using them until you could whip out whatever you needed when you needed it. If you mastered that, of course you'd improve. And when everyone starts using them, we call them "combos" or "strats."

"So, practice and decision-making. For practice, all you can do is repeat, repeat, and repeat until you've got it down. But for decision-making, as long as you're conscious of your strats on a daily basis, you should be able to improve somewhat."

I thought about it and decided she was right.

"And that's where observation comes in?"

Hinami smiled affirmatively. "Yep. Who talks when, and why? What are the relationships in the class? What determines them? When the group decides on what to do together, what factors caused that to happen? I want you to carefully observe, analyze, and verbalize all those things."

"So…I'll be observing people and groups? To get better at decision-making?"

Hinami stood up and walked over to me. Then she leaned down to my ear and breathily whispered, "Hexactly."

"Eeyah!"

Once again, she smiled with sadistic satisfaction as I jumped up, my face burning.

"Anyway, that's the deal. Hopefully, you'll also be analyzing normie skills and weaponizing them for yourself."

All of a sudden, she was talking in her regular tone again, implying I'd overreacted.

Cool and sadistic—that's Aoi Hinami for you.

* * *

"Hey, Fumiya."

Hinami and I had left Sewing Room #2 a few minutes apart. When I got to the classroom, Mizusawa was talking by the back windows with Nakamura and Takei. He casually raised one hand as he called out to me in his smooth voice.

"Hey, Mizusawa."

Consciously imitating him, I smiled casually, raised my hand as nonchalantly as possible, and returned his greeting. Since he already knew I was aping his moves, I didn't try to be subtle. I wasn't at his level yet, but I was getting pretty good compared with before. Or so I hoped.

I wandered slowly to the back of the classroom, wondering what to do.

There was a choice here.

I had to decide whether I should keep walking toward Mizusawa until I joined up with the Nakamura Faction. In terms of EXP, the answer appeared to be yes, and I did want to level up, so that seemed like a good option. But was two whole days together enough to allow me to join their group at school? The overnight trip felt like a separate thing, so maybe I was still forbidden from getting too close to them here. After all, this was me we were talking about.

To buy myself some time, I took smaller and smaller steps as I approached. I had to make a decision. And in the midst of my embarrassing internal struggle, Takei suddenly pointed at me with amusement.

"Farm Boy, what's with the shuffling? What are you, a penguin?!"

"Sh-shut up!" I shot back. Hinami had taught me it wasn't good to sit there and take it all the time, and I'd seen she was right through experience. It was another one of those things you gotta practice. Plus, Takei's normal speaking voice was what most people would consider shouting, so telling him to shut up was instinctive. *Thank you, Takei's loudness. Just… keep it down when you're calling me Farm Boy.*

The wave of normie aggression wasn't going to end that easily, however, and my relief after the comeback was short-lived.

"How do you expect a stupid Fumin to walk?" Nakamura sneered.

I wasn't sure how to respond, but in a situation like this, speed outweighed content. I took a deep breath.

"Who are you calling stupid?"

"Uh, you? Duh."

He fired back immediately. Ugh, typical Nakamura. He had no trouble punishing me with a full combo. But I couldn't give in now. The most valuable challenges are the ones just on the edge of your ability level. I should be thinking of this as a lucky opportunity for snagging EXP.

I was just about to snap back as strong and as smoothly as I could when it happened.

With no emotion, like it was no big deal, Nakamura took one step to the side in the little circle he'd formed with Mizusawa and Takei. There was a space big enough for one more person. It was like…an invitation.

"…Uh…"

What?

Everyone ignored what he'd just done and started talking again.

I was so surprised that I didn't manage a comeback for Nakamura, but I finally picked up my pace and approached the circle with some nervousness.

I stepped into the open space.

The new circle was made of Nakamura, Mizusawa, Takei—and me. What a mismatched group. Suddenly, something touched my butt, and I looked to see what it was. Mizusawa smiled jokingly, his eyebrows raised, and punched me in the shoulder. His expression was definitely teasing, but for some reason, it didn't bother me. In fact, it was comforting.

I looked around the circle again. Mizusawa, Nakamura, and Takei. I could see they planned to keep messing with me…but I didn't sense any malice or any desire to eliminate me from the group. My mind was still fuzzy, but…

I've always lived as a loner, but just maybe…

...if I join a group like this, maybe my life at school will be more peaceful and fun.

Suddenly, I heard a click and returned to Earth. I looked up. There, I saw a cell phone in a bright-red case, its camera aimed at me.

"...Ha! Farm Boy looks so out of it! I'm putting this on Twitter!"

"Hey, wait a second!"

On second thought, there's nothing peaceful about this!

* * *

After a few minutes of desperate pleading, I successfully prevented Takei from posting the photo on Twitter, and the four of us left the classroom. They teased, I argued back, I couldn't muster the courage to mess with them, and pretty soon, we were in the gym. We parted ways to line up in height order, and the opening ceremony ended without incident.

And yes, I was happy to walk back to class alone, but cut me some slack, okay? I can't be training all the time.

As I was sitting down before first period started, I heard someone say "Hey!" and looked over. Izumi was waving her hand next to her chest and smiling a little playfully at me. Her usual friendly expression and actions were a clear reflection of her communication skills.

"Oh, hey, Izumi. It's been a while."

Managing a reply to her sudden attack, I made sure to lift the corners of my mouth and smile as naturally as possible.

"For sure! Not since the barbecue, right?"

For some reason, she looked embarrassed for a second. *Huh?* Then I realized it was probably because the trip had been all about getting her and Nakamura together. After the test of courage, Nakamura had asked her out on a date, which counted as a small success. According to Hinami, she'd told Izumi later about our ulterior motives, and Izumi had been embarrassed but extremely appreciative. Nakamura was the only one who didn't know about it now. Which I think is for the best.

"Oh yeah, you're right."

I got my brain moving. She'd shown some vulnerability. Could I mess with her a little? Usually, my skills weren't up to teasing Izumi, but she'd left herself open. After all, even a dull blade can slice into a stomach. I'll ignore the fact that the blade might be weak as well as dull. Anyway, I reviewed what I knew about Izumi, found the words, and imagined the right tone.

"So? Anything happen with Nakamura?" I asked quietly so no one would overhear me.

Izumi blushed and looked around. "What?! Um, well…"

Success. I guess if I played dirty and made a sneak attack on my opponent's weak point to give myself an advantage, even I could get to Izumi somewhat.

"Um, Shuji said he was busy with family stuff over summer vacation, so we still haven't gone out…"

"Oh, really?"

The conversation returned to normal.

"Yeah…but, um…"

"What's up?"

She glanced down. "Next weekend…we're supposed to go shopping together," she said, clearly enjoying her announcement.

"Oh, wow! Really?"

I was honestly happy for her, so I used my eyes and voice to communicate it as directly as possible. I had a hybrid style—expressing real feelings with skills.

"Yeah…"

Though they'd agreed over summer vacation to go out sometime, they wouldn't actually meet until the second week of September. I had to keep myself from smirking at their typical snail's pace. Still, Izumi and Nakamura were finally going on a date. This was good news—I wasn't wishing death on them or even jealous.

"You did it!"

"Yeah… I've made it this far, so I'm gonna keep going," Izumi muttered, nodding slowly. I think she was talking to herself as much as she was to me.

"Yeah… Well…one step at a time, y'know?"

I did my best to sound genuine. But she took advantage of my slightly emotional mood to make a sudden counterattack.

"What about you?!"

"Um, me? What do you mean?"

"You know what I mean! Don't you have some news from your love life these days, too?"

"Uh, no..." Where did this come from...? I couldn't say I didn't have someone in mind, but I didn't have the courage to tell Izumi about it, so I just looked away. "There's nothing special going on..."

"That was a very suspicious response!"

"Wh-what are you talking about...?"

"Hmm? Very suspicious!"

As usual, Izumi's eyes were glittering at the prospect of romantic gossip. But what even gave her this impression...?

"What are you two whispering about?! Are you talking about sex?!" The voice erupting suddenly from behind me had way too much energy, and I didn't need to look to know who it was. I turned around anyway. Yup. Mimimi.

"Hey, Mimimi! Tomozaki was just saying..."

"Be quiet, Izumi! You don't have to tell her!"

"Oh my god, it *is* sex, isn't it?!"

"No, it's not!"

As the uproar grew, someone in the front of the classroom shouted "Shush!" Tama-chan was pointing sharply at Mimimi.

I hadn't seen Tama-chan since before summer vacation. She was as tiny as ever, her chestnut hair shining. She probably sat in the front because she was so small.

"If you're gonna talk about it, at least keep your voice down!"

This tiny girl's scolding didn't have much force by itself, but her posture was threatening enough. Mimimi being Mimimi, she shivered with happiness at Tama-chan's reproach.

"Ooh... A good tongue-lashing from Tama-chan is just what my tired body needed..."

"That's *not* what I meant!"

It was fun watching Tama-chan energetically complain. Of course, Mimimi was ten times as energetic as Tama-chan. What was with those two?

"Ah, my Tama-chan deficiency is being replenished!!"

Mimimi bounded over to Tama-chan for a good old-fashioned bear hug. Business as usual.

"Hey, stop it, Minmi!"

Ignoring Tama-chan's attempts to resist, Mimimi nuzzled her face happily into her friend's neck. When she was content, she lifted her head slowly and stared at Tama-chan's face with a strangely serious expression.

"Oh, Tama..."

She touched Tama-chan's nose experimentally, then looked down.

"...What?"

"You haven't...?"

She paused sorrowfully. Her gaze darted around anxiously, and her mouth opened slightly like she wasn't sure what to say. *Wh-what's wrong, Mimimi?*

"What...?" Tama-chan asked nervously.

Mimimi looked her in the eye again and slowly began to speak.

"...You haven't changed your bodywash, have you?" she asked forlornly.

Tama-chan was silent for a few seconds. Then she pointed fiercely at Mimimi, her face bright red. "What I smell like is none of your business!!"

"Nya, nya!"

Mimimi grinned broadly and stuck out her tongue. Was I just imagining it, or was Mimimi getting more perverted by the day? If I didn't watch out, this could go way too far.

Anyway, once the initial uproar was over, the two of them settled into their usual routine of scolding each other and chatting cheerfully. Whew. I was just thinking the fuss was over and I could get back to my peaceful routine when I noticed a gleam in Izumi's eyes.

"Getting back to what we were talking about... Do you have any romantic gossip for me, Tomozaki?"

"Um, no, it's..."

Another thing to watch out for: Izumi's tenacity on this kind of topic.

* * *

I managed to evade Izumi's interrogation until the first-period bell rang. As Kawamura-sensei walked in, Izumi abandoned the conversation with a satisfied smile. I guess she's happy just to talk about that kind of thing even if she doesn't get any real information?

"Okay, take your seats, kids. The bell's ringing!" Kawamura-sensei said briskly. Man, she's a fighter.

Everyone stopped talking and silently sat down for long homeroom, the first class of the second semester. Kawamura-sensei straightened the stacks of half-size paper on her desk and started on an important-sounding lecture.

"...You may all still be second-year students, but college entrance exams are on the horizon. I assume you each studied on your own over summer vacation, and you'll soon be starting classes here at school to prepare as well. Today, I'll be giving you a career survey and explaining your elective options."

Completing her speech with her usual confidence, she handed out the stacks of paper to the first student in each row. The survey that landed on my desk basically assumed we were all going to university, which was obviously the goal our school had for us. We might be in Saitama Prefecture, but Sekitomo High was still a respectable college-prep school.

"Please select your classes based on which exam subjects you'll be taking..."

Instead of following the gen ed curriculum, we were shifting into test-prep mode. Kawamura-sensei explained that the class would be divided into several sections based on our elective subjects and that we'd be studying the content of the upcoming exam intensively.

After all, the exams were coming up in a little over a year. I wasn't awful at studying, but I hadn't made any concrete decisions yet about the future. *Guess it's time to give some serious thought to my career. So far, all I know is that I want to try to get into university.*

Kawamura-sensei finished up her explanation and gave us some time to fill out the surveys and turn them in. Once we were done, her expression relaxed as she flipped through them.

"...Right. We've got some extra time, so let's discuss the sports tournament. It's coming up in three weeks!"

"Yes! I've been waiting for this!" Takei shouted cheerfully. The class giggled. *Wow, a couple of words, and he got a laugh.*

I thought about stealing some of his skills but quickly realized it would be hard to copy him directly. I mean, if *I* said *I've been waiting for this!* everyone would just be confused. He was building on his existing character, while my existing character was a loser and mostly invisible. Sad. I guess I better focus on observation for now, like Hinami told me.

"Yes, Takei, we've all been waiting eagerly for this. But what we need to do now...is pick the girls' and boys' team captains."

Kawamura-sensei wrote the word *Captains* on the blackboard.

"Their main job is to attend the captains' meetings. The captains from each class will get together to decide which grades will be playing which sports, and they'll create a schedule for using the courts. The captains will also help get the courts and equipment ready on the day of the tournament and manage the teams during the matches. Basically, they're in charge of the business side of things. We need one boy and one girl for the role. Any volunteers?"

"I'll do it!"

Takei's hand shot up so fast, it seemed almost like a reflex. Another ripple of giggles passed through the class. I'm pretty sure this is less a skill for Takei than an inborn gift. It feels like the defining property of his character. You could sum him up in one word: *simple.*

"Okay. If there aren't any other volunteers, then Takei will be the boys' captain."

"Yes! I'm gonna get us soccer!" Takei pumped his fist, burning with an innocent sense of duty.

"Except last year, you lost at rock-paper-scissors, and we got stuck with volleyball," Nakamura jeered. The class laughed. So Takei ran for the position two years in a row...

Wait. That jab was interesting, actually.

If I thought about it systematically, this was an application of the *messing with people* skill. Nakamura was just teasing one person, but because he did it in front of a group, he got some laughs.

I'd practiced this already, so this might be within the realm of possibility for me. The problem was whether I had the courage to do it publicly, and there was a chance that everyone would just think it was really weird... *Yeah, I'm not touching that yet. Better watch and practice some more first.*

"Who cares? Hey, Aoi! I choose you to be my partner!"

Takei energetically gestured at Hinami.

"Hmm, but I don't think I can. Right, Kawamura-sensei?"

She tilted her head playfully, nailed Takei with a smile, then looked at the teacher.

Takei stared at Aoi in shock. What kind of trick was that? Her ability to get guys tied up in knots was archery-on-horseback territory. If Hinami had a trait, hers was *shape-shifter.*

"That's right. Starting this semester, Hinami will be serving as student council president, so unfortunately, I'll have to reject her nomination as captain."

"No way!! I only volunteered because I thought Aoi would be the girl's captain!"

The whole class laughed again. Were they laughing because he was being so honest? I was good at saying what I thought, too, but I didn't have the skills yet to give it such a comical spin. If I wanted to copy him, I needed to practice giving a happy-go-lucky delivery.

That aside, Takei really was crazy about Hinami, huh? On the barbecue trip, he'd been dying to pair up with her in ping-pong, too. Or was she just that popular?

"Ha-ha-ha. My condolences," said Kawamura-sensei. "Do you want to quit now?"

"No way. I'm doing this!" Takei pumped his fist again.

"Ha-ha-ha. Then the job is in your hands, Takei. Which means we have a boys' captain... Now how about the girls? Anyone?"

Kawamura-sensei surveyed the class, but the girls just glanced around at one another. I did my best to pay attention to their glances and the general atmosphere. This time, I was observing the overall mood instead of their individual skills.

One thing I knew was that the warmth generated by Takei's joking earlier was steadily cooling. Honestly, captain wasn't such a desirable job to start with. From Kawamura-sensei's explanation, it didn't sound very fun. In fact, it sounded annoying. Takei was just a special case.

I half expected Mimimi or someone to throw up their hand like Takei had, but no one made a move. Mimimi was a much more thoughtful person than her ditzy persona would suggest. The class's forward momentum ground to a halt.

Suddenly, Mizusawa let out a dramatic sigh that cut through the silence like a knife, and he turned toward Takei.

"Aw, don't worry, man. Don't feel bad just because no one wants to be your partner."

"Wait, what?! Is that why no one is volunteering?" Takei shouted in a tone that betrayed both his anxiety and sadness. The guys in the class burst into laughter at his emotional reaction. Aha, this was the same method Nakamura had used earlier. But damn, Mizusawa's delivery was perfect. I wouldn't expect any less, of course.

I looked around at the girls. About half were laughing, but the other half were just smirking a little. Huh. It wasn't a super-serious situation, but I think they were having a hard time relaxing enough to laugh when the possibility remained that they'd have to be captain. Makes sense. Everyone hates annoying jobs.

What about the queen of our class, Erika Konno? I glanced in her direction. She was slouched in her chair with her legs crossed, bored and neutral as she examined her fingernails. Wow. What an impressive aura. Her trait would be *queenly dignity*. I looked away quickly, since I'd be in big trouble if our eyes met.

"No volunteers for the girls' captain?"

Naturally, no one responded.

"...Hmm. In that case, we'll decide later. The tournament isn't for a little while, and the captains' work doesn't start until...looks like next week. If anyone decides they want the job between now and then, please sign up. Moving on..."

But just as Kawamura-sensei was about to wrap up the discussion...

"...What about Yuzu?"

The queen's voice rang out sharply.

"Um, me?" Izumi floundered at being called out so suddenly.

"You were captain of Class 2 last year, weren't you?"

"Um, uh-huh...," Izumi said hesitantly, rubbing the nape of her neck like she didn't know what else to do.

"I thought so! You already know how to do it, so like, why not?"

"Uh, um..."

Konno knew she had the logical upper hand here, and she was pressing her advantage, while Izumi was refusing to give a solid yes or no.

Yeah, I recognized this dynamic.

When I went to Izumi's house last semester, she talked about how she always went along with the mood, even if she didn't want to. That was probably how she ended up with the job last year. And given how good Erika Konno was at bending the mood to her will, I was expecting Izumi to cave and take the job again.

But sometimes things don't go how you expect them to.

"No, but..."

"What?"

Izumi shifted her gaze nervously. "It's just...I don't want to be captain this year..."

She answered quietly but honestly.

This was fairly surprising. I hadn't noticed a strong will in Izumi's eyes, but she'd managed to resist Erika Konno's grumpy, controlling gaze. Last semester, when we went to her room, she'd told me she wanted to stop letting the mood control her, and she was gradually making that wish a reality. I was mesmerized. On the surface, it seemed like a tiny, maybe even weak rebellion. But in that action, I saw concrete signs of her will to grow, however slowly.

There was a brief silence, and then Erika Konno looked away from Izumi, annoyed.

"Oh. Okay," she replied a bit snappishly, resting her cheek on her hand.

Izumi let out a soft breath, the tension draining from her hunched-up shoulders. Her eyes looked a little moist. That really took her outside her comfort zone, and she'd almost cracked. *Nice work, Izumi.*

I felt myself relaxing, too, and I was sure I wasn't the only one, now that the crisis had been averted. Erika Konno truly was a powerful mood manipulator to be able to create so much tension out of just a few words and glances. As the tension dissipated, I started to wonder where in the world that power came from.

A moment later, however, Erika Konno shot her second arrow. Her cheek still resting on her palm, she absently twirled a piece of hair between her fingers.

"Well, how about Hirabayashi, then?"

"...Huh?" Hirabayashi-san was too startled to say more than that. She had long black hair with thick bangs, and she was one of the quieter girls in our class. I'd seen her with friends, but not often—she was a loner, as they say. Why had Erika Konno named her? I tried to figure it out, but I couldn't come up with an answer.

"Come on, Hirabayashi. You should do it. You're good at, like, setting up and stuff."

Erika Konno gave a short, vaguely mocking laugh, which made it clear the supposed compliment was code for *You're boring.*

Then, as if they were following Erika Konno's silent orders, the members of her group started chiming in.

"She does seem good at setting up."

"What's that mean anyway? Ha-ha."

"I hope she does it, for the team."

This wasn't outright coercion, but they were definitely pushing her in that direction. And in the background, Erika Konno was watching over it all. Invisible violence inflicted through the mood. Damn.

"Someone has to do it, after all."

"Exactly! And we have to choose the right person for the job!"

"Seriously, though, how is someone good at setting up? Ah-ha-ha."

Erika Konno's groupies were getting all worked up over this as she looked on like it was completely normal.

Hinami defined *mood* as "*the standards for right and wrong in a particular situation.*" As I observed the situation based on the "rules" she'd taught me, I started to draw some conclusions.

What Erika Konno and her followers were doing was probably very simple. They were using the existing mood of the class to indirectly attack Hirabayashi-san. Most likely, one of the norms in our class dictated that it was bad to be boring and practical. By that standard, plain people had a lower status than loud attention-seekers.

By labeling Hirabayashi-san as being *good at setting up*, Erika Konno was using that norm to indirectly belittle her and affirm their hierarchical relationship. And then after establishing her superior status, she was trying to push an annoying job on her.

Now that I'd laid it all out in words, I really did not like this norm.

I kept thinking and observing quietly. How could I intervene using the skills I had? Could I change the mood? I searched for a way to combine my observations with my existing skills so I could change the outcome.

But the more I thought about it, the more I felt like my skills weren't up to the task. I mean, I couldn't even smooth out the mood of the class in a normal situation. How was I supposed to suddenly leap over this high hurdle?

It was frustrating, but I decided to keep watching silently. It would have been one thing if I was the only one at risk, but if I screwed this up, Hirabayashi-san might get hurt, too. Better play it safe.

"How about it, Hirabayashi? Yes or no? If you're not gonna do it, say so."

Erika Konno made the full-court press, probably to make the mood impossible to resist. Her groupies pushed, too, murmuring, "Yeah!" and "Come on!"

Izumi was the only member of their group who didn't say anything. She just stared at Hirabayashi-san with worry.

Hirabayashi-san seemed to hesitate for a moment, but she finally gave up, smiled faintly, and raised one hand next to her face, her arm pressed tightly to her side.

"Okay…I'll do it," she said to Kawamura-sensei.

"…Hirabayashi. You don't have to do it if you don't want to. Plus, we don't have to decide today. We have plenty of time."

But despite Kawamura-sensei's serious, scolding tone, Hirabayashi-san shook her head.

"Um…it's fine. I'll do it."

She smiled weakly again, like she was trying to ward off her own discomfort.

"…Well, okay." Kawamura-sensei didn't seem fully convinced, but she accepted Hirabayashi-san's offer. I guess she didn't have much choice when Hirabayashi-san herself was volunteering. "So we're going with Takei and Hirabayashi for the captains?"

"All good here! Can't wait to work with you, Miyuki-chan!" said Takei. He had the spirit, if nothing else.

"Uh, um, right… Me too."

Hirabayashi-san's brief smile then was real.

So that was what happened in the long homeroom on the first day of the second semester. I spent the whole time silently observing for my assignment, and what I saw wasn't pretty. Mood maneuvers are like boxing for normies. Honestly, this kind of thing is way outside my wheelhouse, but I guess it's necessary for conquering life?

On the upside, I could take some pointers from Takei's people skills, like the way he remembered Hirabayashi-san's first name and acted so friendly to her. The only possible reason such an idiot could be so socially successful must be that there was a part of him that was impossible to dislike. To continue the boxing metaphor, he was like the mascot character who only showed up in the ring between rounds. *I'm rooting for you, Takei.*

* * *

It was break time after first period. The bell rang, Kawamura-sensei dismissed us, and everyone wandered over to hang out with their respective group of friends. I glanced to the side and noticed Izumi was still sitting in her chair, staring dejectedly at her desk. I didn't want to just leave her, so I decided to say something. *Lately, I think my training has been starting to merge with my own feelings.*

"...Izumi?"

"Huh? ...Oh, Tomozaki."

Returning to Earth with a start, she tried to hold on to her smile as she turned to me. I didn't exactly tease her, but I had that sense in mind as I took a step closer to her.

"You thinking about...what just happened with Hirabayashi-san?"

"Um...yeah," she said awkwardly. "...Could you tell?"

"Yeah, kinda."

Izumi sighed and lowered her voice. "It's just...I wasn't sure what to do."

"Yeah?"

Izumi glanced quickly at Erika Konno, then smiled darkly. "What do you think I should have done?"

"...Hmm."

I could tell she was feeling bad about not doing anything to rescue Hirabayashi-san. So was I.

"That's tough. There wasn't much we could have done."

Izumi nodded. "Yeah... It's not like Erika was doing something so bad that I could have told her to stop."

"...True."

I agreed. Like Izumi said, all Erika Konno and her friends actually did was nudge Hirabayashi-san; they didn't force her or threaten her. Plus, all they were pushing her to do was be captain of the sports tournament. Yeah, it was a hassle, but it wasn't *that* much work. If it was so horrible to push someone into that job, then why did Takei volunteer for it himself? Once again, we'd return to the fact that Takei was an idiot.

"Konno didn't force her to do it."

"Yeah..."

It would be easy to condemn her if she'd clearly threatened Hirabayashi-san, but ultimately, the main reason Hirabayashi-san ended up with the job was because she herself said she'd do it. The mood had created an invisible coercive force, but that invisibility made it hard to condemn.

"I guess all you can do is avoid making too big a deal of it and see how things go," I said.

"Yeah, I guess so," Izumi answered, looking down and smiling. "But..."

"But...?" I prompted.

She nodded and then continued. "If I just became captain myself, the problem would be solved."

"...Oh." Yeah, that would be one way of rescuing Hirabayashi-san.

"But then that would be bad for me on a personal level."

"Um, bad how?" I asked, not completely sure what she meant.

"Well, it would be easy for me to take her place, but..."

"...Yeah?"

Izumi pressed her lips firmly together for a second. "But that's exactly what Erika wanted."

Now it was coming together. I thought back again to what Izumi had told me at her house.

"...Oh."

She didn't like how vulnerable she was to the mood.

"I want to change that part of myself...so I've been making more of an effort in these situations, you know?"

She sounded shy and a little ambiguous. I think by "these situations," she was including the *Atafami* match between Nakamura and me in the old principal's office. I could still remember Izumi clumsily but insistently rebelling against Konno's crew when they were attacking Nakamura.

"Yeah," I said, nodding intently.

Izumi lowered her voice a little more. "And then today...I tried it again when I told her I didn't want to be captain. Man, she was scary! Did you see her eyes?!"

"I was getting scared just watching!"

"Right?!"

We both giggled. Wow, laughter in a normal flow of conversation. I had to admit it felt good that we were laughing without even trying. I was also enjoying how the conversation seemed kind of secret. *Wait, what am I talking about?*

"Didn't I do a good job of standing up to her? C'mon, give me some credit here!"

"Fishing for compliments much? Didn't you almost start crying?"

"Shut up! Seriously, though, Erika is *terrifying* when she gets like that!"

As I rode the wave of conversation, remembering to tease her here and there, something occurred to me. I was a bottom-tier character, but I wasn't the only person struggling to grow one day at a time. Izumi was going through the same thing as a normie.

"Aaanyway…I think you *are* changing little by little."

"What?! Really?"

I really meant it, and Izumi's eyes lit up. *S-stop! Back up a step! I'm still not used to that normie smell—soft, slightly sweet, full of teen spirit… My magic defense is practically zero.*

"Um, uh," I mumbled incoherently.

"Uh," Izumi said, examining her palms. "You did say…that it wasn't too late for me to change."

"…Oh yeah."

When she opened up to me that one time, she'd mentioned her troubles with the mood, but also that she believed that would never change. And I'd disagreed.

"Ever since then, I've been trying when I can."

"…Oh, uh-huh."

Izumi nodded and smiled playfully. "Plus…*you* were the one who let her have it that one time. It was so cool, I had to step up my game, too!"

"Oh, um, thanks."

I managed to reply even though she'd just dropped a "cool" on me and scrambled my brain. The ability to deliver these surprise attacks is definitely a normie trait. They have a big impact on us bottom-tier characters, even when we know there's no meaning behind it. It's super effective!

"But…anyway. If I gave in and agreed to be captain, I'd be going right back to how I used to be. I guess I didn't want that to happen."

"…Makes sense."

Like she said, if she gave in to Erika Konno's manipulation of the mood to make whoever she wanted the captain, that would be the same as giving in to the mood itself. Especially if Izumi didn't want to be captain.

"Yeah," Izumi said softly, sighing with deep exhaustion. "...People can be such a chore. Especially in groups."

Her words startled me. All the struggles I'd been through to complete Hinami's assignments, including this current one, spun around my mind like a carousel, and before I knew it, my mouth was moving almost against my will.

"They are... They really, really are...," I said as all the emotions of the past few months welled up inside me.

"Geez, you don't have to make it *that* big a deal!"

Izumi seemed a bit weirded out.

* * *

Since it was the first day of the second semester, we got out of school at noon. Hinami had told me she couldn't meet after class, so I was planning to head straight home. According to the extremely businesslike LINE message she'd sent during break, she was having lunch with Mimimi and Tama-chan, and it would be hard for her to get away.

I was planning to get home as quickly as possible and use the extra time to practice *Atafami*, but twenty minutes or so after school, I instead found myself at the game center near the station by our school.

"Holy shit! Farm Boy's good!"

Takei was standing behind me, cheering as I played. Nakamura was sitting in the opposite arcade cabinet and playing against me, and Mizusawa was standing behind him.

Yes, Nakamura's henchman Takei had kidnapped me as I was getting ready to head home and taken me here (unharmed) to the slightly smoky Cruz Game Center.

"Damn, Farm Boy, you're kind of a freak at this!"

"Shut up, Takei."

"Ouch!"

As I coldly snapped back at Takei, I racked up another victory. It was getting really easy to fire back at him. An idiot like him was practically holding up a neon sign saying *Just go for it!* Sure made practice easier. Training-mode Takei.

The screen in the cabinet in front of me refreshed. I took a deep breath and looked around. Unlike the arcade I went to sometimes in Omiya, this was a small place, probably independent. It seemed like a hangout for the semi-rough crowd at the local high schools—in other words, I did not belong here.

"…Shit, dude, you're way too good. It's so… Eh. It's whatever."

Nakamura scratched his head in irritation as he stood up and walked over to my side with Mizusawa. Judging from the round we'd just played, Nakamura had spent a decent amount of time practicing this combat game called *Dogfight 4*—but not as much time as I had. Maybe that was why he wasn't bashing me as hard as usual for kicking his ass. He hadn't even insulted me, so that was a big step forward. Sad that it *is* a big step forward, but I'm gonna ignore that.

Nakamura plopped down beside me. The run-down game center's beat-up chair creaked as he spread his legs wide apart, invading my space. Damn. He acted like it was totally natural to be so domineering. I squeezed my legs together. The pressure of the situation made me nervous, but I focused on not stammering like an idiot.

"I *did* practice…"

"Huh," he said without looking at me.

Mizusawa seemed impressed and peered at the screen. "So you're good at games aside from *Atafami*?"

"I'm okay. This one's pretty famous."

From what I could tell after a quick glance around the arcade, all the games they had were famous. They probably went for the usual suspects because they didn't have a lot of space. I could probably beat Nakamura at any of them—after all, I'd put in a ton of solo practice. Ha-ha.

"I've never lost to any of the guys here. You practice too much, man. Go outside once in a while."

Nakamura was pushing me around, like always. He really was a force to be reckoned with.

Still, I made an effort to observe, as Hinami had instructed me. When I did, I realized his comment to "go outside" had a similar structure to Erika Konno's comment about Hirabayashi-san being "good at setting up."

By labeling Hirabayashi-san as *good at setting up*, she'd established Hirabayashi-san's inferior position according to the standard that dictated plain and practical were bad.

Similarly, Nakamura had treated me as plain by saying I should "go outside," using the same norm as Konno to put me in my place. Nakamura at least accepted that I was good at gaming, so his comment felt a lot milder than hers, but the structure was identical. Must be a typical normie strat.

"N-nah, I like gaming more."

Given that I was getting Hinami's help to become a normie myself, I wasn't sure if I should be quite so proud of it, but what else could I say? That's genuinely how I feel, and that's not about to change. I'm not about to give up what I like. I'm going to beat this game of life as a gamer and have a good time doing it.

"Whatever. Okay, Fumin, this one's next."

"Oh, okay."

"You're running him ragged, man."

"Go, Farm Boy, go!"

For all my worrying, they brushed over my declaration of nerdiness like it was nothing, and Nakamura proceeded to use me as his practice partner for a while longer.

* * *

It was already past six. We'd taken a break for lunch at a Gusto diner nearby, but other than that, we'd been battling the whole time. We'd already been playing for five hours, in fact. *Seriously?*

"Shuji, how much longer are you gonna go?" Mizusawa asked with a cynical smile.

"Yeah, Shuji, let's get out of here soon," Takei added, sounding a little unhappy.

"You guys go home first. I'm gonna hang here a little longer."

"I'd like to go home, too…"

I felt like Nakamura was assuming I'd stick around as his training partner, so I made sure to correct that idea. I mean, if I stayed any longer, my parents would really start worrying.

"Oh yeah? Okay, see you later."

"Later."

Surprisingly, he let me go. I thought he'd tell me to stay. Well, okay then.

"Ready, guys?" Mizusawa said with a sigh, as if he'd guessed what was up with Nakamura, and then he led Takei and me out the door of the game center. I glanced back as we left. Nakamura was sitting expressionless in front of the game cabinet, his arms crossed, illuminated by the light of the screen. There was something sad and vulnerable about his face in the light of that dim, old-fashioned game center.

After we left, the three of us headed toward the train station. The afternoon had been hot, but now the heat had settled in favor of a comfortably warm breeze. Mizusawa sighed quietly once more.

"Looks like it's happening again."

Takei swiveled his head toward Mizusawa and pointed at him in agreement.

"I thought so, too! You think they had another fight?"

This was an interesting conversation.

"All he can do is wait it out. Yoshiko's super strict."

"Think it'll last for a while?"

I didn't recognize the name Mizusawa had mentioned, so I decided to ask.

"Who's Yoshiko?"

Was there a girl in our class named Yoshiko? If so, why would they mention her?

"Shuji has a complicated family situation. His mom is really overprotective—one of those helicopter parents. If he gets bad grades, messes around too much, or stays out too late, she gets *super* pissed. And she's tough to beat on the best of days."

"R-really?"

So Yoshiko was Nakamura's mom. Was calling her by her first name a normie thing? *But now that I think about it, I remember somebody mentioning that his mom was scary when we had the Nakamura-Izumi strategy meeting at my house.*

"I'm guessing they're fighting right now," Mizusawa said, checking the train schedule on his phone.

"A fight, huh…? But won't he make it worse by staying out late?"

Mizusawa smiled innocently. "You'd think so, right? That's the frustrating thing about Shuji."

Takei threw his head back and guffawed in agreement.

"What do you mean?"

"He's stubborn," Mizusawa said warmly. "When they fight, Shuji stays out on purpose."

I smiled cynically.

"So…he doesn't want to see her 'cause they're fighting? Or does he want to make her worry?"

"You got it," Mizusawa replied, pointing at me gracefully.

I sighed. So basically…

"What is he, a little kid?"

"Ha-ha! Seriously!" Mizusawa laughed loudly. "He'll stay at a friend's house or go home really late so he doesn't have to see his parents."

"Th-that is so childish…"

Still, it was also in character… I pressed my fingers into my forehead, a little frustrated with him myself. Takei grinned, as if to match my gesture.

"You're spot-on, man! He's so childish, I worry about him sometimes!"

"You're hardly one to talk," I shot back.

"Ouch!"

I'd said what was on my mind in a natural tone. I'd practiced enough by now that I was able to do it fairly smoothly and naturally. This must be what Hinami was talking about when she mentioned repeated practice. It kind of felt like reflexively responding with an uppercut to an attack from the air.

"Why's Farm Boy being so mean to me today?"

"Ha-ha-ha. But come on, you really can't talk."

"Takahiro, you're getting in on this, too?"

That was basically the tone of the conversation on the way home, and I actually felt fairly comfortable.

* * *

We split up, and I went home. My mom complained about how unusually late it was, but I just ate dinner and headed for the bath. As I soaked in the hot water, I reflected on the day.

I'd gone to the arcade after school with some normies, and we'd hung out till night, messing with one another. I'd been careful to observe, but I hadn't forced myself to do anything weird simply for the sake of an assignment, either. Still, strangely enough, school had become a little livelier for me.

Actually, the change was so dramatic, I could never have imagined this a few months ago. But I knew better than anyone else that this seemingly personality-transforming change was made up of one tiny, inevitable step after another. I wasn't using a continue, a cheat, a shortcut, or anything else like that. I'd just advanced a little further each day, until I turned around and realized the starting point was far behind me.

But if that was the case…

…there was someone else who had come much further than me.

Just how long had Aoi Hinami been walking this path, and how far had she gotten?

Right now, she was so far ahead of me that it was hard to even imagine where she had started. But at some point in the past, the one and only Aoi Hinami must have been standing where I was now. It was probably so long ago that her footsteps had worn away. To get from here to there, she hadn't used a time warp or magic or anything like that. She'd just walked straight ahead, one step at a time, like I was doing.

But there was one major difference between Hinami and me.

For me, each step of this journey, from the feel of the earth beneath my feet to the landscape stretching out before me, was new, exciting, and full of enjoyment. That's what kept me moving forward.

But not for Aoi Hinami.

It seemed like for her, moving forward in and of itself was the goal. She didn't enjoy the journey, she didn't look around at the new scenery, and she didn't look back at the starting point. She kept her gaze fixed on the goal, and she forged ahead almost like a machine. At least, as far as I could tell.

What had allowed her to keep at it for so long?

I had to wonder.

2

The best games make reconnaissance fun

"That's a good sign."

It was the next day, and we were in Sewing Room #2. I was telling Hinami how I'd been able to mess with Takei fairly easily after school at the game center.

"Yeah?"

She nodded, looking fresh as a daisy. I've mentioned it before, but it bears repeating that she goes to morning track practice before our meetings. She didn't look tired, and she didn't smell sweaty—in fact, she smelled good. What planet was she from?

"You were able to mess with him and keep up a conversation without making a conscious effort, right?"

"Yeah."

"You've probably realized this yourself, but this just proves my point. You couldn't tease him even if you wanted to before, but after a little practice, you can do it now without any conscious effort. It's virtually the definition of skill attainment."

I nodded, savoring her words.

"…Huh. I guess you're right."

I'd sensed it myself: My skills were naturally coming out during real-life battles.

"How is the observation going? Have you made any discoveries?"

"Well, now that you mention it…"

I told her what I'd noticed about the mood-manipulation war when we were deciding who would be the captains of the sports tournament, and how Erika Konno had reaffirmed the hierarchy with the *plain equals bad* norm and her "good at setting up" comment. Also, how Nakamura had used a similar structure when he told me to "go outside once in a while."

"...So I figured that was how normies did things."

For some reason, Hinami seemed happy when her eyes met mine.

"Nice one, nanashi."

"Huh?"

Smiling with satisfaction, she nodded a couple of times.

"Mood is a pretty abstract concept, but you've been able to analyze it to some extent because I've taught you the definition. And now that you've learned the rules, you can overcome your handicap as a nerd and deduce the hidden structure behind mood all on your own... Yeah, those are nanashi-level accomplishments."

"Really...?"

I wasn't sure why, but she'd just given me one hell of a compliment. I did get stuck on the phrase *handicap as a nerd*, but it was the truth, so I decided not to let it get to me. Poking at that would just lead to unnecessary pain.

"Listen. That ability is the privilege of people who are able to observe the rules from the outside and avoid getting sucked in."

"From the outside?"

"Yes. We've been through a lot, but I think you're essentially..."

She whispered the words *on this side*. Before I could react, though, she hustled the conversation on to the next topic. She really did run the show.

"Your analysis is generally correct. The norms state that being boring or quiet is bad, so people establish their position by showing off. And by labeling other people as the opposite, they lower those people's standing and establish a hierarchy. It happens in every group; it's just how things are done."

She was exposing the ugly side of daily life in the classroom, but all in a flat, logical tone. I nodded and replied:

"My analysis didn't go quite that far, but one reason I became a loner to start with was because I hated that custom so much... But I'm planning to jump into the ring now," I said, whipping up my morale. I've come to believe that if I want to win this game and enjoy it, I've got to fight according to the rules of the mood. I'll decide as I go if climbing in there is worthwhile. But until I find something that allows me to destroy or ignore the rules of that ring, I have to follow them. At least, if this is a good game.

"Right. If you're a true gamer, you'll engage with the rules instead of run from them."

Hinami's words made sense.

"Yep. The rules decide the conditions, and you pick up your controller and hack your way through."

Hinami nodded happily.

"Exactly."

Only a pair of gamers would be able to see eye to eye on this so quickly.

"...So what's today's assignment?" I asked, changing the subject.

Hinami looked at me suspiciously. "Did you suddenly decide to ask about assignments yourself from now on?"

"Huh?"

Once she mentioned it, I realized I'd done the same thing the day before, too. "Oh, no, not on purpose, but...I guess I'm just feeling motivated."

Back when all this began, I never would have asked for assignments so eagerly. She hadn't forced me into this, of course, and I'd even taken the initiative to some extent, but a part of me was still passive. Or maybe I should say I'd gotten my butt kicked a little. And grabbed. Literally.

Now I could see more clearly, and my motivation to complete my daily assignments was definitely higher. When I asked myself why, the answer was immediately obvious.

"I think...it's because of what happened between us a little while back."

"Huh...? That gave you motivation?" she asked skeptically.

"It's like...I really saw the value of working at this. Like I realized what my ultimate goal was or something. I mean, it's like getting absorbed into a game I like and having a good time."

"You're talking about the whole 'what you really want' thing again, aren't you?" Hinami drew her eyebrows together suspiciously.

"Yeah. Everything clicks for me now, so there's nothing holding me back."

Hinami looked at me with an emotionless, oddly direct gaze.

"I really don't get you," she said softly.

"...You don't?"

The reason I got a little flustered was because she seemed less unconvinced and more uncomprehending. When I couldn't explain, though, she gave up and went back to her usual self.

"Your assignment for today—for the foreseeable future—is to do some special training on mood."

"Oh, okay."

I tried to shift my mind into assignment mode while keeping up with what Hinami was saying. So an assignment about mood. Thinking about the future, it seemed like a crucial topic.

"You probably understand that if you want to be a normie, you need to have more rights than other people and more of an ability to speak."

"Yeah. You were talking about something similar when we went to get a present for Nakamura, right?"

Hinami nodded.

"I told you then that another important issue is responsibility. Basically, your rights only extend as far as you can take responsibility. This is an important foundation for moving the group. And you have to level up until you can take more responsibility for more things. It's not something you can do overnight."

"Huh."

Made sense. If you want the right to influence other people's actions, you've got to take responsibility. But that's a hard thing to do.

"But there's a way to manipulate the group on the spot and increase your rights instead of using the rights you already have. What's needed for that is—"

"The ability to manipulate the mood," I interrupted. Hinami glared at me. Then she sighed.

"Hexactly," she mumbled. *Why so grumpy?* "Groups move based on the mood. That's why in reality, even people who don't have the right to influence the group can seize control when they have the ability to manipulate the mood. And if you do that on a regular basis, you expand your rights and slowly inch up the hierarchy."

"...Gotcha."

If you want to gain the right to manipulate the group—if you want to approach boss level—it's important to develop those abilities. Just like she told me before.

"That's why, starting today, your training will focus on developing the ability to manipulate the mood."

"Okay! Bring it on."

I put up my fists like a boxer, and Hinami held up a finger next to her face.

"As for what that *is* exactly... Well, the sports tournament is coming up, right?"

"Um, yeah..."

"Your assignment starting today is..."

She paused for a few seconds.

"...is to get Erika Konno's group motivated to participate in the tournament."

I knew what she was saying grammatically, but I couldn't actually parse it into a concrete image.

"...Um, well, you're right that they don't seem to care much...," I stammered.

"They sure don't. And you probably don't have any ideas on how to motivate them, right?"

"Nope," I said, shaking my head. She'd identified my worries perfectly.

"That's fine. Because that's the essence of this assignment."

"Huh?"

Once again, I wasn't following.

"Okay. For all your assignments so far, I've told you clearly what to do, such as 'talk to a girl' or 'mess with Nakamura,' right?"

"True..."

"The goal then was to improve your basic abilities, so completing your previous assignments would develop your skills. I set it up that way."

"Uh-huh."

Up till now, I didn't have to think much. And since I'd naturally improve as long as I did what she said, that was fine.

"But this time, I want you to build your ability to manipulate the mood, which requires more complex, flexible thinking. And you need hands-on training to develop those thinking skills."

"...Which is why you're telling me to motivate Erika Konno's group to participate in the sports tournament."

Hinami nodded before replying:

"You know that motivating them is going to require complex trial and error, right? That's your training."

"...Okay."

I nodded, satisfied with her explanation. We were shifting from assignments that required action over thought to ones that focused more on application, which demanded careful deliberation. And this would improve my understanding of mood.

"So considering what strategies to employ is part of my training?"

Hinami nodded again.

"Yes, but...you're already practicing one skill needed for this assignment," she said pompously.

"I am?"

"Oh, you haven't figured it out?"

Seeing my confusion, she raised her eyebrows in amusement.

"Observation," she said, a sadistic grin playing on her lips. The assignment from the previous day was linking up with today's conversation.

"...Oh. That's what you're talking about," I said with a smirk. Looks like my previous assignment of observing the group would be playing an important role. Which meant Hinami had today's assignment in mind when she gave me the one from the previous day? Damn, she's efficient.

"Right. And starting today, I want you to prepare by observing and analyzing the situation."

"You've planned this out very carefully..."

Now that she'd laid it all out, though, it was simple. In *Atafami* terms, I'd practiced combos and other refined manipulation techniques and gotten decent at them. Now it was time for a test battle or two to help me get better at those techniques in the field.

"But observation alone won't always be enough, so in those situations, you can act as you see fit… Actually, I think this might be your most gamelike assignment so far."

"Oh yeah?"

For some reason, Hinami gave me a meaningful smile.

"Mm-hmm. Anyway, there's no rush to complete this assignment, and I'd like you to spend some time on it. You can start by spending the next two weeks or so quietly observing."

"Okay…got it."

Now that I understood the assignment, I tried to think about what I'd need to do in order to complete it. Nothing came to mind. I gripped my head.

"…My assignments are getting harder again."

Hinami was definitely enjoying my distress. What a jerk.

* * *

I left Sewing Room #2 and headed to class. First period hadn't started yet. As I looked around, I noticed something was different from usual. I walked over to Takei and Mizusawa, who were talking by the window.

"Nakamura's not here yet, huh?"

He was always here by this time.

"Nope," Mizusawa said, turning toward me. "I think he's out today."

"Huh."

Could be. Fall was coming, which was cold season.

"I bet you anything he's skipping!" Takei said cheerfully.

"Really?" I asked.

"Remember what we told you about Yoshiko yesterday? That's probably why."

"Huh," I said, a little confused. He was skipping school because he argued with his mom? Gutsy move. Or maybe just childish.

"This is Shuji we're talking about, so I'm sure he'll come back when he feels like it."

"R-really?"

Based on their casual tones, this was par for the course. I'd kind of already realized he lived by his own rules. Oddly enough, I'd never noticed him missing class before, but that just showed how unobservant I'd been in general. This would be obvious if I'd paid the least bit of attention.

Another normie in our class approached us. He was a tall guy with short black hair who looked like an athlete from the way he moved. Uh-oh, this was an anomaly. *Um, I'm fairly sure his name is Tachibana. Not sure what club he's in, but I'm guessing basketball.*

"Shuji's out today?"

Mizusawa made a silly face.

"Yeah. I'm betting he got in a fight with his mom," Mizusawa replied in a jokey way.

"Again?"

Tachibana laughed. Apparently, Yoshiko was famous.

Huh, interesting. Add just one unfamiliar person to the group, and everything gets ten times more stressful. On the other hand, this was a good chance for me to get some EXP, especially since I was already used to hanging out with Nakamura, Mizusawa, and Takei. *Okay, then. Time for me to lean into this conversation. Better start by introducing a topic.* I made an effort to sound casual despite my nerves.

"Uh, does this happen a lot? I mean, Nakamura fighting with his mom?"

Tachibana looked at me and nodded.

"Yeah. You didn't know that, Tomoyama-kun?"

"It's Tomozaki, not Tomoyama..."

"Oh, really? Ha-ha, sorry!"

My momentum was gone after a single shot, while Mizusawa and Takei started cracking up.

I made it through another couple minutes of awkward conversation with the normie Tachibana before the bell for first period rang. I was beat;

I needed to give myself some kind of reward for this trial. *Atafami* marathon when I get home!

Since this was still the second day of the semester, every period was full of busywork like going over summer assignments and doing little quizzes. The real work would start after the weekend, next Monday.

By the end of third period, I was struggling with my assignment.

I was supposed to start taking steps today toward motivating Erika Konno's group to participate in the sports tournament. But how the hell was I supposed to do that?

I mulled it over constantly during class and breaks, but no answer appeared. According to Hinami, observation was essential, but I had no idea what exactly to observe, or how.

Surely the one and only Aoi Hinami would never give me an impossible assignment.

I had the skills I needed for this. *So what am I missing? Information?* And then I remembered something: Hinami had said this was my most gamelike assignment so far.

...Hmm. What do you do in a game when you need info? Oh!

This assignment was *an RPG*!

When the bell rang at the end of third period, I turned to the seat next to me.

"...Izumi?"

"What's up?"

I waited a beat before continuing. "I wanted to ask you about Erika Konno."

Yup. When you don't know how to advance in an RPG quest, there's only one thing to do: collect information in a town. If Erika Konno was the dungeon boss I had to take down, that meant I should check out the town for intel on her weaknesses and how to defeat her. So the first person I should talk to was one of her close associates. Wow, this suddenly felt like a game. *Hah, it's kinda fun now.*

"Huh? About Erika?"

Izumi measured me up with her glance. I guess it made sense; I had no discernible connection to Erika Konno, and now I was asking this.

Okay, so life *is* a little harder than other games. The villagers in an RPG would even randomly volunteer information like *Speaking of which, I've never heard of a sand dragon attack on a rainy day...* And then it's perfectly obvious the dragon's weakness is water.

"No, it's just...she seems pretty meh about the tournament coming up."

"What are you talking about?" Izumi asked, but she looked amused. I had to choose my questions better. This was reality; there was no list to pick from. "I mean, of course she is. She thinks it's lame to care about this stuff."

"Ha-ha...I could tell."

I laughed cynically. I already knew all this.

"What do you think would make her care?"

"Hmm, I dunno," Izumi said, thinking for a minute. "That's a tough one."

"Yeah, I figured..."

I sighed. Lots of people in this village were suffering at the hands of the boss, so it was unlikely they knew what her weaknesses were. If even her close associate didn't know, this was going to be hard.

Nevertheless, Erika Konno wasn't the kind of boss I could take down with ordinary attacks at my level. If I didn't find some kind of exploit, there was no way I could beat her.

"...But why are you so interested anyway? Where did this come from?"

"Uh, um..."

Figures she would ask—but I had a good excuse ready and waiting.

"...Well, Hirabayashi-san is gonna be captain, right?"

"Huh? Uh, yeah." Izumi tilted her head quizzically. Even that ordinary gesture was cute coming from her—I guess her normie power could account for that. It was like adding an elemental charge to an ordinary attack. Light elemental, to be specific, so it hit me extra hard.

"I mean, this isn't really her thing anyway, and I bet it's even harder when Erika Konno is dragging her feet. Especially if you're a girl."

And especially, especially if you're a loner without many friends. Believe me, I know.

"Oh...yeah," Izumi said, nodding. Maybe she'd experienced what I was talking about. "The job is gonna be a huge headache if Erika's not into it."

She grimaced, maybe because she was imagining the situation. This didn't bode well.

"Y-yeah…"

Something in her reaction told me that the world of girls was a lot harsher than I'd imagined.

"So anyway, I wanted to do something to help Hirabayashi-san… Plus, I want to have a good time without worrying about, like, class politics," I said, wrapping up my prepared excuse. It wasn't a lie, though. I really did want to make life a little easier for Hirabayashi-san, the victim of the most recent mood attack. Plus, I honestly wanted to have fun, considering I was enjoying school more overall lately. I mean, as much fun as I can have when I suck at sports.

As I looked Izumi in the eye and waited for her answer, I noticed that her round eyes were starting to glitter with childlike excitement. Huh?

"Oh man, I get you!!"

"Yeah?"

I wasn't sure what to make of her hyperenthusiastic agreement. What was up? Lowering her voice a little so no one would hear us, but still in just as excited (and intense) a tone, she continued.

"I *love* the sports tournament and the culture festival, and I want them to be as much fun as possible. Otherwise, I feel like I missed out… If nothing else, it's just more fun to have fun, y'know?"

"Yeah, true," I said. Her passion was contagious.

"But it sucks when you don't have everyone in class on board, right? Even for me, and I'm close with Erika. But for someone like Hirabayashi-san… it's gotta be even harder."

"…Right."

It would be hard to really cut loose, knowing what she was going through.

"So I've been wondering if there was any chance Erika would actually take this seriously."

"Oh, you have?"

If Izumi wanted to enjoy the tournament, but the queen was acting like enthusiastic people were uncool, she'd have a harder time enjoying it. Izumi hung out with Hinami's group sometimes, but her main clique was Konno's. And then there was Hirabayashi-san, at the bottom of the hierarchy. Yeah, groups were complicated.

"Yeah, but Erika wasn't into it, and I didn't think I'd be able to ignore her. I'd just about given up..."

That was a surprise to hear.

"You couldn't ignore her? Seems like you could just hang out with Hinami or someone at the tournament..."

Izumi shook her head with a very sour expression.

"No way! She'd be super pissed if I ditched her to go have fun with someone else... Girl politics are the worst!"

She hunched her shoulders and curled in on herself.

"W-wow." I nodded. I couldn't fully imagine how she was feeling, but I had a good idea.

"So I was gonna give up, like I said, but...you're amazing!"

"I am?"

Suddenly, she was praising me. I had no idea why. What did I do?

"I mean, I could see someone trying to have fun behind her back, or covering their tracks with some excuse, but who would ever think of trying to get *her* into it?"

"Oh...okay."

It made sense now that she said it. People didn't usually attack head-on like this. It probably felt refreshing to someone who wasn't used to it—me included. I'd simply inherited the strategy of my master, Hinami, as part of an assignment. Izumi wasn't really praising *me*, because I hadn't actually done anything special.

"But it's gonna be hard. What would make her excited?"

She sank into thought. After a few seconds, she frowned and got a distant look in her eyes. I think her brain might have been overheating.

"Uh, um... Is there anything that Konno normally cares about? That would be useful to know." I tossed her a life preserver, and she brightened right up.

"Well, she puts a lot of effort into her appearance. I know some good clothing stores, so she's always asking me to go shopping with her. She tries on tons of outfits and asks me how they look and stuff."

"Huh..."

I hadn't expected to discover this side of Erika Konno. I'd figured she would act like any clothes she wore were gorgeous. The veil of secrecy concealing the dragon called Erika Konno was slowly lifting to reveal data that would form the foundation of my strategy.

"Also, she's super picky about makeup. She tries out tons of different brands and studies the techniques and stuff... Don't tell anyone, but I buy the Wet n Wild–type stuff a lot of the time. If Erika knew, she'd make fun of me for sure..."

"Wet n Wild...?"

Izumi looked confused by my question for a second.

"...Oh, I just mean the cheap brands!"

Ah, okay. I just got some experience in being the idiot. Or not. I'm so ignorant about normie culture, I stumble over the unimportant stuff, preventing the conversation from moving forward. One of the downsides of being a bottom-tier character, I guess.

"Sorry, go on..."

"Anyway...that's about it. She's just really into anything related to beauty!"

Izumi nodded a few times.

"I see. Beauty, huh? That's gonna be hard to connect to a sports tournament..."

"True," Izumi said, smiling wryly.

"But if we start with that..."

I started to put this new information into the context of the rules I already knew, but this was tough.

After a minute or two, Izumi made a solemn suggestion.

"How about offering some Chanel lipstick to whoever wins?"

"I...I think that's a little too on the nose..."

It was like a tacky direct-marketing proposal. Normies really have big imaginations...or maybe that's just Izumi.

* * *

The next day was Saturday. I didn't have school, but I did have work. It was my first day at the karaoke place since I'd finished training.

I stood in front of the bathroom sink at home, styling my hair—which I'd been getting cut regularly at the place Hinami had told me about—using the techniques Mizusawa had taught me. Wearing the clothes Hinami had taught me how to choose, I got ready for work. Yup, when it came to my appearance, I just might be able to fool people.

As I was doing a final check in front of the mirror, someone suddenly flew up behind me and shouted "Hey!" which caused me to jump.

"Shit!" I said, turning around. "...Oh, it's you?"

"Uh, yeah, obviously," my sister said, pouting grumpily.

"What?"

She looked me up and down.

"You look...put together. What, got a date?"

I wanted to tell her it was none of her business, but since I wasn't actually going on a date, I decided not to. But I was happy for the compliment.

"No, work."

"No way!" she shouted, mouth gaping. "You got a job?!"

"Yeah."

She was acting like this was the end of the world.

"My weird brother has a job?"

"What's that supposed to mean? I'm capable of getting a job on my own."

Okay, that might have been a slight overstatement. Hinami was the one who'd told me to get a job, and this felt like a big deal to me. Even now I was super nervous, but I was trying not to show it. I'm a big brother; we're stubborn.

"Oh, *oooookaaaaaaay.*"

She stared at me. What? What was with her?

"It's a karaoke place in Omiya. I can get you in for half price if you ever wanna come," I said, raising my eyebrows. Damn. Why am I bluffing now? I'm a big brother; it's just how we are.

"I don't."

Shot down. She doesn't take me seriously, does she?

"Okay...," I mumbled.

"What happened with that girl from before?" she asked, changing her tone.

"G-g-g-girl from before?"

Stuttering like a bottom-tier broken record, I feigned ignorance.

"The one who asked you on LINE to go buy a book together."

"You read that...?!"

"Better than letting you hole up in your room forever and miss your chance to answer, right?"

"Uh...," I said, easily giving in to her. After all, she'd saved my butt by reading that message from Kikuchi-san and getting me to do something about it. If she hadn't said all that stuff to me after Hinami and I argued, I probably would have missed my chance to get together with Kikuchi-san. This big brother is still weak.

"So did you go out after that or what? Any girl who would ask *you* must be pretty special, so you'd better be good to her."

"Sh-shut up. It's none of your business," I bluffed, even though I secretly agreed with her.

I'd seen Mizusawa's mask and argued with Hinami, and I'd made up my mind not to confess any love I didn't actually feel. I would stay true to my own feelings when I interacted with people. After the day Kikuchi-san and I went to the bookstore together, I hadn't talked much with her. I felt it would be insincere of me to ask her out. But even if I didn't want to say I liked her as part of an assignment, and even though I still didn't know if I *did* like her that way, it didn't change the fact that she was an important person in my life. I was deeply indebted to her for teaching me something incredibly valuable.

In which case, yeah, my sister was right.

I'd learned to use my skills of expression to convey my genuine feelings. If someone was important to me, then it was necessary to take steps to express that sentiment and make sure I didn't lose that person. In this case, my sister lit a fire under my butt and reminded me of something I should have known.

"None of my business, huh?" she asked. Her tone was teasing, but at the same time, she was staring into my eyes. I felt like my soul was being examined.

"No…my little sister wins this round. I offer you my most sincere and humble thanks."

"I'll take it."

I jokingly overacted my thank-you, but in my mind, I thanked her a little more sincerely. *Thanks, Sis.*

* * *

"Good morning!"

It was a little before noon. Following the bewildering custom of saying *good morning* even when it wasn't exactly morning anymore, I walked into the karaoke place.

"Hey, Tomozaki. Training's over now, so I'm counting on you, okay?"

"Yes, sir!"

The manager, who I'd seen a bunch of times during training, was putting the pressure on. I took the key from him and headed for the changing room. I quickly threw on my uniform and returned to the front desk.

"Go scan your veins. I showed you how, right?"

Scan your veins probably sounds super weird, but actually, it's just an electronic time card that uses the patterns of the veins in your finger to identify employees. People at work are always using special lingo like *wipedown* and *upsell* and *tapster* and *no guests,* which sound like normal words at first. It's really confusing. By the way, those terms apparently mean *cleaning a room, offering food or drinks, the person who makes drinks,* and *no customers in the building.* The more you know, I guess.

"Yes, you showed me!"

"Okay, then go scan in and come back here. Today, I'll start teaching you how to man the front desk."

"Will do!"

With a spring in my step, I got to work learning my job.

* * *

Several hours had passed.

"Morrrrning."

The extremely lethargic greeting came from my coworker, Narita-san—Tsugumi Narita. She was the first person I met when I came for my interview. She's a year younger than me and goes to a different school, and all I remember about her is that she's super laid-back about everything.

"Hey, Tomozaki-kun. Been a while."

As a bottom-tier character, I'm incredibly grateful any time someone I haven't seen in a while remembers my name, but it weirds people out, so I tend to hide it. So I pretended to be calm.

"Morning, Narita-san."

I tried to emulate Mizusawa in my response and channel that mature aura. Which reminds me, Mizusawa called Narita-san "*Gumi*," but I couldn't quite go that far in my impersonation.

"Hardly anyone here calls me Narita-san. Feel free to call me Gumi, okay?"

It was like she'd read my mind, but that's just how she was. Last time I saw her, she told me not to speak so politely to her, robbing me of the time I needed as a low-level weakling to mentally prepare myself for that degree of familiarity. I wish she'd stop bullying us weaklings.

But I'm a man, after all. And I'm a gamer who made up his mind to beat the game of life. I'll show the world I can walk the path of strife. The old me would have compromised by calling her *Gumi-chan* instead and congratulated myself for moving past *Narita-san. Well, I'll take it a step further!*

"Uh, okay. Looking forward to working together, Gumi," I said, playing it as cool as I could. *How do you like that? Don't I sound like a great Mizusawa knockoff?*

"Me too!"

Blissfully unaware of the storm of self-examination and determination in my heart, Narita-san—I mean, Gumi—easily accepted my use of her nickname. Yeah, normies were good at this kind of thing. I'd made a special effort just now, but it would be tough to ditch the *-san* or *-chan* every time. I felt more uncomfortable than I'd expected calling her just Gumi. *From now on, it'll be Gumi-chan.*

* * *

Several more hours passed.

"Drinks are ready. Can you take them out, Tomozaki-san?"

"Be right there!"

At first, it didn't bother me.

"Can you extend the time for Room Fourteen?"

"Okay!"

But little by little, it started getting to me.

"Customer! Tomozaki-san, do you know how to sign people in?"

"Um, yes, I learned it today."

"Great, then can you do it? If you have any questions, ask the boss!"

"Will do!"

This first-year, Gumi-chan…

"Have you checked the bathrooms?"

"No."

"Then since you're free now, can you do it?"

…didn't lift a finger.

"Also, the dishes are piling up, so go ahead and wash them when you get a chance."

"…Um…"

"Yes, what is it?"

Thinking about how Mizusawa would tease someone in a situation like this, I'd come up with my complaint in advance.

"Do your job."

I delivered my line in a slightly theatrical tone. *D-did that come out okay?*

"…You got me, huh?"

"At least pretend to be sorry."

Her response was so quick, it was almost refreshing. I had to smile, but I still tried to make my own comeback as stern as possible. *O-okay, she isn't being weird about it, which must mean I didn't screw up.* She didn't laugh, so it wasn't a complete success, but practice makes perfect. She reminded me of Takei, actually. It felt okay to talk to her more harshly than I would with other people, which made interacting with her slightly easier.

"Well, I do try to work as little as possible," she said nonchalantly.

"...Sheesh."

I couldn't help sighing. No way was I ready for an opponent of this caliber.

"What? What's wrong, Tomozaki-san? Do you have to use the bathroom? Go whenever you need to; that's what I do. Also, don't tell anyone, but when the boss isn't around, I help myself to the drink bar in the kitch—"

"No, I'm fine."

I just couldn't keep up; she was too lazy for me.

An hour later, I was in one of the karaoke rooms.

"Whew..."

I put my phone in my pocket and took a deep breath. It was five o'clock, and I was exhausted from my first day of posttraining work. The boss had told me to take a break, so I'd slipped into this room about thirty minutes earlier and collapsed onto the sofa to recharge. My exhaustion was about 20 percent physical and 80 percent mental. I had an hour for break. Work would start again in half an hour.

Having a job was surprisingly tiring. There wasn't all that much to do—I probably had more downtime than busy time—but interacting with strangers as an employee was tough for a bottom-tier character. The biggest source of stress was easily Gumi-chan's behavior.

As I was chugging down my free drink and trying to relax, the door suddenly opened.

"Nice work out there, Tomozaki-san."

"Huh? Oh, uh, you too."

Recovering from my shock, I managed a reply. Gumi-chan waltzed in, plopped down next to me on the sofa, and melted into the cushions.

"Wh-what?"

"I just got off. Was gettin' kinda tired, so I wanted to sit for a little before I got changed," she said listlessly, resting her full weight, including her head, against the back of the sofa and the wall. She looked like a snake. I didn't know a person could let go of their energy that fully.

"Oh…okay."

I'd witnessed her whining about exhaustion multiple times today when literally all she had been doing was standing. It's rare to find someone with less energy than me, the scrawny, indoor beanpole. Or maybe the issue was mental, not physical?

"Wait…you're done already?" I asked, suddenly realizing she'd arrived at work after me.

"Yeah. I usually don't work more than three hours. I'm a rare character!"

She sat up slightly and fluttered her hands back and forth.

"What's that about? Is it because you get tired?" I asked, smiling cynically.

"Exactly!" she said, smiling and sticking her pointer finger in the air. I couldn't figure out what was so good about that, so I decided to ask her, in as teasing a tone as possible.

"Why do you sound so happy?"

"I mean, aren't *you* tired? I don't wanna bust my butt to make money."

"Yes, I get that, but…"

Once again, I wasn't sure if I'd succeeded or failed, but I supposed it was fine because what mattered was effort.

"Right? My creed in life is to avoid work whenever I can! Thanks in advance for your help!"

"Oh, uh…huh."

What was that supposed to mean, "thanks in advance"? More important, her approach was the polar opposite of my current attempt to beat the game of life, which gave me pause. *Avoiding work whenever you can, huh?*

"What? You don't agree?"

Gumi-chan looked at me with her round, innocently questioning, but somehow still listless eyes, waiting for my answer. It was a tiny pause, but the way she caught it was another sign of her normie status.

Since she asked, I might as well tell her what I was thinking.

"Well, in my opinion, life is more fun when you put your whole heart into it and move forward…," I said a little shyly and hesitantly.

Gumi-chan looked surprised. "Huh. So you're one of *those* people."

"Wh-what's that supposed to mean?"

She crossed her arms. "You know! The people who are super into the chorus festival or the culture festival or the sports festival."

"…Ah."

Now I got her point. Up till last year, I wasn't that type at all, but now I absolutely was. I was even trying to get the girls in my class to be more excited about the tournament.

"You may be right," I said.

"Plus, I can tell you made a real effort to learn the job here. I'm proud of you."

"What are you, my mom?"

"I'm proud of you"? Really?

"Like I said, I just don't want to bust my butt over that sort of thing. I want to relax, y'know, not let people burn me out. Soooo—thanks in advance!"

That seemed to be her catchphrase, delivered at a mysteriously pleasant tempo. She offered so many opportunities for comebacks that I'd definitely be able to get some practice in. I found my joking tone again and said:

"You're a hopeless case, aren't you?"

"Guilty as charged."

"Ha-ha."

Once again, I was unsure if I'd succeeded or failed. Was her key trait the ability to absorb all teasing? Or maybe my teasing was just ineffective? In either case, this was tough. She wasn't simple like Takei.

"The culture festival is coming up at my school. Everyone in my class is so excited about it—it's exhausting."

"That so?"

I realized something. Here was a girl who had no interest in class events… This could be the perfect opportunity to gather some intel. I thought about what I should ask her. *Okay, time for round two of RPG reconnaissance!*

"You don't have any interest in participating?" I asked, searching for the right words to draw out the answer I wanted. *Wish I could just pick from a list.*

"Nope."

"Yeah, but…isn't there anything that would make you want to join in?"

I was collecting information in the village to take down a unique superboss—that is, to get Erika Konno excited about the tournament. From what I could tell after talking to Gumi-chan, she had attributes similar to those of a boss. On the surface, she and Erika Konno were completely different, but they sure knew how not to give a damn. This was like asking a lizardman how to take down a dragon.

"Wait, why are you asking me? Are you trying to make me try harder? Ugh, just don't," Gumi-chan said, for some reason covering her chest with her arms. *Come on, you don't have to act like I'm harassing you! I just asked a normal question.*

"Oh, no, it's not that…"

"Then what is it?"

She glared at me sullenly. What was her deal?

"Um…," I floundered. Ultimately, I decided to go with the truth. "We've got this sports thing coming up at my school, and some of the girls are really dragging their feet."

"…Oh. Gotcha."

Gumi-chan removed her arms from her chest, apparently satisfied with my explanation. What the hell? Did she equate someone suggesting she actually do something with sexual harassment?

"I thought you might have some ideas on how to get people interested."

She looked at me with slight disgust. "I know your type."

"Huh?"

She scrunched up her brows.

"Working isn't enough for you. You try to drag everyone else along with you, too. You're dangerous. Like an alien or something."

"Don't you think that's a little much?"

NARIT

She was coming on strong, but I managed a comeback.

"Nope. I can't even imagine thinking like you, Tomozaki-san. It's bizarre. But whatever. If you need to know what I think, it's no skin off my nose."

"R-really?"

"Yep. I'm probably a total alien to you, too, so I can teach you the ways of my planet. Think of it as a cultural exchange," she said, winking at me.

"Um, okay…"

This was getting weird. *Is this RPG set in outer space?*

"Anyway, I'll be your expert on apathy," she said, grinning. Weird. Who's that proud to be the go-to source for apathy?

* * *

"Ohhh, that's really annoying."

I'd just given Gumi-chan a quick rundown of Erika Konno's personality, the power structure of our class, and the tournament captain Hirabayashi-san. She shook her head, rubbing her temples.

"Yeah."

She looked me in the eye. "I bet Erika-san had it out for this girl Hirabayashi-san."

"Oh…"

I'd suspected the same thing. There had to be a reason she went straight to Hirabayashi-san after Izumi turned down her command to be captain. I had no idea what that reason might be, though.

"Yeah, you were screwed the minute that girl became captain. Your queen is not gonna want to be a part of this."

"Queen…" The word fit her perfectly.

"Plus, from what you've told me, she seems to live on Planet Apathy, too."

"Planet Apathy… Then I must live on Planet Effort?"

"Ah-ha-ha, something like that," Gumi-chan said with a carefree chuckle. "Anyway, you're gonna need a big shock to the system to get her on board."

"That's what I was afraid of…" I sank into thought.

"Looks like you've got your work cut out for you." Gumi-chan laughed. Why was she suddenly so happy about my suffering?

"But what do you mean by 'a shock to the system'?"

She thought for a moment. "Cost performance is key. That's true for me, too."

"Um, what do you mean?"

"Okay, here's an example. You know how I feel about work, but I have this job, right? Why do you think that is?"

Tough question. There must be something she wanted.

"Is it related to cost performance?"

"Yep! Very good!"

She gave me a round of applause. Oh boy.

"So…what's your point?"

"Compared with other jobs, the pay here isn't bad, and it's pretty fun, right? And the schedule is super flexible."

"Oh, really?"

All I'd done was follow Hinami's instructions to apply here, so I had no idea how this job compared with other places, but given that Mizusawa worked here, it must not be terrible. He had good instincts.

"The point is, you can't do nothing all the time. You have to put in a little effort here and there. Like, you need money in order to take it easy most of the time. And when inhabitants of Planet Apathy *do* have to work, we choose the option that requires the least effort and gives the best results."

"Ah… That's what you mean by cost performance."

"Exactly."

So that explained why Gumi-chan was working at a fun, well-paying job with a flexible schedule to earn the money she needed.

"And you think Erika Konno is similar? Because she doesn't think it's worth the effort?"

"Yes! If you want to motivate the queen, you need to make it worth her while."

She accompanied this original conclusion with an unclouded smile.

"Yeah…"

"But my guess is your queen's apathy isn't nearly as extreme as mine, so it's a worthwhile endeavor."

"You think so?"

Gumi-chan nodded in general agreement. "That's my guess anyway. I mean, she acts all bossy in class, right? That means she has a lot of emotional energy. Being bossy and snobby is exhausting. If you *really* didn't want to waste energy, you wouldn't bother."

"Huh… Makes sense."

Her argument was persuasive. If I imagined her in Erika Konno's place, I could easily picture her complaining and giving up the throne in no time.

"I'm sure she wants a lot of things, unlike me. I don't have a selfish bone in my body. My only desire is to not do anything," she said, flopping over onto the table. She was practically a liquid.

"Hmm…"

"Look, people make an effort because they want things. I'm a negative example—I don't have anything I want, so I don't put forth any effort."

Still flopped on the table, she turned her face toward me, smiling listlessly as she delivered her oddly convincing argument. Maybe she really was an authority on apathy.

"But what does our queen desire?" I asked.

Gumi-chan sighed loudly. "Oh, Tomozaki-san, listen to yourself."

"Huh?"

She looked me in the eye solemnly. "You think I'd know what other people want? Nope, dude. Can't relate. Obviously."

She was being strangely forceful about this, but her words were completely unhelpful.

"Oh, okay…"

"Welp, time for me to take off. I hope I was helpful!"

"Yeah, uh-huh."

I was powerless to stop her, and I just waved as she slipped out the door. But okay. The end of our conversation was unsatisfying, but hearing her unique insights had been valuable. Payoff for effort—that was the key. *Geez. She just does whatever she wants...*

* * *

It was just after six. I'd finished work and was standing in front of the Bean Tree sculpture at Omiya Station, waiting for someone. The station was technically indoors, but the entrances and exits were all wide-open, so it felt like the place couldn't decide whether to be air-conditioned or not. Saitama in general seemed to have trouble deciding what it wanted to be, though, so I guess that made sense. Maybe the train company had designed the place this way on purpose.

People were streaming through the rows of ticket gates in an unending current. I watched them absently as I waited, breathing deeply to calm myself down. *Okay, feeling better.* I gave myself a little pep talk, and when I took another look around, I registered a mystical, saintly presence approaching from the east exit.

Yes. Kikuchi-san had arrived.

"Oh...!"

Noticing me, she trotted over and gave me a modest smile.

I'd been thinking about a lot of things—a lot about Kikuchi-san in particular, partly because of what my sister had said to me. It had been a wild couple of weeks—the stuff with Hinami, and about assignments, and about what I really wanted—but that didn't change the fact that I was indebted to Kikuchi-san. She'd taught me so much, and I didn't want to lose her.

When I thought about it, I realized we both had jobs near Omiya Station. If we both got off work at the same time, we could meet fairly casually. I'd sent her a LINE message during the first half of my break that afternoon, and she'd written back immediately that she got off an hour after I did.

Well then, just say it! I told myself, and I'd summoned my courage and asked her out. And now here we were. And yes, I did report all this to Hinami.

"Um...hi, Tomozaki-kun."

"Oh, um, hi, Kikuchi-san."

She was dressed a little more casually than usual, and around her was a feather mantle protecting her from the evils of the human world—I mean, no, a lightweight black cardigan that she wore to keep off the sun. She wore a short-sleeved, white button-down with a collar, as well as a skirt the deep-green color of leaves from a billion-year-old tree. A single scrap of that fabric could cure all disease. Well, probably.

"Thank you…for inviting me to meet up," she said, wrapping her arms around herself and looking away from me. My heart quivered at her solemn words, which echoed like gospel.

"Um, uh-huh," I said, suddenly extremely aware of my own heartbeat. "…Are you hungry?"

"Oh, yes, I am, I think."

"Then…"

I racked my brain for a good place to go, figuring I should take the lead. *Um, what's near Omiya Station…?* I started to panic. *Shit.* My mind was a blank. Knowing Kikuchi-san, even if I suggested Tenya, she'd probably say something like *Oh, tempura is so delicious,* but what would that say about me as a man? The phantom Hinami-san in my mind was eyeing me with disdain. *"You're kidding, right? Only a real loser would take a girl to Tenya on a date."* But this isn't a date!!

Why didn't I look something up beforehand? I'd decided to stop wearing a mask of confidence or whatever, but right now, I think it would have been better to have a restaurant in mind. There was the place Hinami and I had gone for lunch that time, but I vaguely remember glancing at the dinner menu and thinking the prices were insanely high, so that was out. What about the café Kikuchi-san and I had gone to after buying books? Could you go to the same place twice in a row? What's your verdict, Hinami-san? I decided to save that as my backup.

A random diner or something would be okay, too, if I knew of one, but there weren't many around the station. Or maybe there were, but a high school loner like me wouldn't know where to find them. Was there one in that building that had a Loft in it when I was in junior high? Loft was neat. I liked the Sakuraya by the east exit, too. *Okay, snap out of it!* I was freaking out.

Hoping I might be able to recover with a map app or something, I opened my phone and noticed a LINE message from Hinami. There was a URL attached. *Hmm?* I clicked on it, and it led to the website of an affordable café a few minutes' walk from Omiya Station's east exit.

"Damn..."

"...? What's the matter?"

"Nothing..."

Unable to explain my surprise to Kikuchi-san, who was looking at me with confusion, I led her to the café Hinami had suggested. This was getting close to telepathy.

* * *

We arrived at the café, and the interior turned out to be a quirky blend of nostalgia and attention-grabbing Western-style decor. It had a big potted plant sitting next to an antique-looking, red sofa. The cluster of stone sculptures of nude women, the colorful bottles on the table by the register, and the replica *Mona Lisa* on the wall were trademarks of typical Western showiness, but they lent a certain retro feel at the same time. It wasn't so much a Western place as an old-fashioned Japanese café decorated to vaguely resemble one.

"This café has such...unusual energy."

"...Yeah."

Kikuchi-san herself had way more unusual energy than this café, but I knew better than to say it aloud and make her think I was a creep.

"The atmosphere is wonderful," she said with a smile that made me feel like I'd been touched by the breath of an archangel.

"Um, yeah...it is."

I felt a little shy and out of place here, but I silently thanked Hinami for her choice. *You saved my butt...*

We sat down across from each other at a table and stared at our menus.

"They sure have a lot to choose from."

"Wow, you're right..."

Kikuchi-san flipped through the menu excitedly, her face relaxing into a smile.

"I think I'll get…the Napolitan pasta," I said.

"I'm going to have the *omurice*."

I remembered that she picked the same thing the last time we ate out.

"You really like *omurice*, don't you?"

Kikuchi-san giggled happily at my slightly teasing tone, which I could manage smoothly now thanks to repeated practice. The move was like my uppercut now.

"I didn't even notice!"

"Oh, so you're on autopilot until you've ordered?"

"Pretty much!"

We shared a laugh. As always, the time I spent with Kikuchi-san was quiet and natural, but warm. Enjoying this comfortable mood, I called the waiter over and ordered for both of us. I was trying hard to take the lead. Once that was over, I drank some water and took a breath. Kikuchi-san was gazing at me with an affectionate smile more beautiful than *Mona Lisa*'s on the wall.

"Thank you so much for coming with me to buy that book last time."

"Oh, no, thank you…for everything."

"…It was nothing."

"…Yeah."

The atmosphere was peaceful and solemn, like the early morning over a silent, frozen fairy lake deep in the woods where all the animals were hibernating.

"It's so quiet in here," I said, glancing around at the decor. "I like how calm it is."

Kikuchi-san smiled. "You've been working hard, haven't you, Tomozaki-kun?"

"Wait, what?" I asked. This conversation had taken a turn.

"You have so much energy these days," she said gently, her fingers laced together on top of the table. She was right.

Two days had passed since the semester started. I'd been talking with Nakamura's group, whispering with Izumi, and messing around with Mimimi and Tama-chan. Life was happening all around me. I guess it was obvious to outside observers, too. All the more so because Kikuchi-san sat diagonally behind me in class. It was also possible she was blessed with the ancient gift of clairvoyance.

"Yeah, you could be right. Or maybe I'm just louder." I smiled awkwardly.

"You think so?" she asked simply, looking at me with her startlingly honest eyes.

I looked inside myself once again. There was a part of me that had a tendency to run into self-deprecation and self-flagellation...but I couldn't do that. I had to be honest.

"Lately...I've been enjoying it," I said. Kikuchi-san smiled happily.

"That's wonderful."

She always stripped my heart bare, but it felt warm and comfortable. Once again, I realized how at home I felt with her.

Our food arrived, and we chatted about nothing at all as we ate. After a while, I decided to ask Kikuchi-san something I'd been wondering about.

"Um..."

"Yes, what is it?" she asked calmly, after taking her time to chew and swallow the bite of food in her mouth. Very like her. If she'd asked *me* something midbite, I'd gulp it down in a panic and start stuttering.

"Um, you know Erika Konno in our class?"

"Konno-san?"

I nodded. "What do you make of her?"

I still hadn't collected enough information on Erika Konno. Izumi had told me what interested her, and Gumi-chan had told me about her desires—which meant she would act based on cost performance or opportunities. But I needed more to complete my assignment.

That was why I wanted to get Kikuchi-san's input. Asking as many people as possible for information about a boss was an ironclad rule of RPGs. Kikuchi-san saw straight into people's hearts, and besides, I had a feeling that fairies living deep in the woods knew a lot about how to take down dragons.

"That's a hard question to answer..."

"Oh yeah, sorry, um..." Yeah, that was too abstract. I thought about how to reword it. "What I meant was, when do you think she decides to care about something? Like right now, we're getting close to the sports tournament, but she seems to have zero interest in taking part, right? So I was wondering when she would be interested."

Kikuchi-san nodded with understanding.

"Oh, so you want to know what motivates her."

"Yeah… Yeah, that's what I mean."

Motives—that was a good way to put it. Which reminded me, Kikuchi-san had asked me before what motivated Hinami to work so hard, saying she was a writer and wanted to understand.

"Well…hmm. This may not sound very kind, but…"

"Yeah?"

Kikuchi-san rested her cheek on her hand and looked down slightly, like she was unsure how to phrase this. After a few seconds, she peered up at me. Her enchanting eyes, like two lakes dappled with magical, sparkling flower petals, melted my thoughts completely away. Finally, she parted her delicate lips.

"She doesn't want people to look down on her—I think that's a big motive for her."

She was being careful and unassertive, but she'd cut right to the core of Erika Konna. *She doesn't want people to look down on her.* Harsh, but not impossible to understand.

"She doesn't, huh?"

"Yes…"

Maybe because Kikuchi-san realized she'd said something kind of mean, she was slumped more dejectedly in her seat than usual. Right now, she was as adorable as a squirrel.

"I can see that…" I was convinced.

For instance, you could say that by creating and enforcing the *boring is bad* rule, Erika Konno was protecting herself from being at the bottom of the hierarchy. Izumi had said her interest in makeup and clothes was a sign that she cared what other people thought about her, and that fit, too.

Even her massive attitude and the way she pressured others was a part of it. In that light, all her actions appeared to come from a single source: not wanting to be looked down on. I just had one question.

"So…why would that make her act this way about the sports tournament?"

The tournament created a clear ranking between classes. If she was so concerned with how people saw her, wouldn't it be more natural for her to try to reach the top?

Kikuchi-san hesitated again.

"It must be…because if she acts like the tournament is already stupid, it won't matter if we win or lose… People still won't look down on her."

"…Oh."

Once again, she cut straight to the heart of things. I was convinced. If you made fun of the tournament, no one would laugh at you when you didn't win. After all, trying was uncool to begin with. I was following her logic now.

Given how quickly Kikuchi-san had responded, I realized she must watch our classmates on a regular basis, her careful analysis allowing her to sum them up perfectly. She was doing the *group observation* assignment Hinami had given me. Huh. I was learning a lot by asking so many questions. This really was like an RPG.

"But Konno-san does care about her friends, and I think she can be more honest than she realizes, so I don't think she's a completely horrible person…"

"Yeah."

Kikuchi-san seemed to feel guilty for what she'd said, but the way she was frantically trying to walk it back was a little funny to me.

Anyway, I kept thinking about her original point.

"So she heads off the problem by acting like it's stupid… Interesting."

"Yes…"

I was connecting the dots with Gumi-chan's comments about desire and the cost performance of effort. Erika Konno wanted to avoid effort whenever possible. At the same time, she didn't want people to look down on her. But as long as she belonged to our class, she had to be at the top in controlling the mood or else she risked being looked down on. That must be why she put so much effort into her appearance and actions.

Because she had to.

If she didn't, she wouldn't get what she wanted. On the other hand, the sports tournament was another story. True, putting in real effort and winning a top spot was one way to fulfill her desire. But most likely, *the cost performance of that option was poor.*

That was because she could simply create a norm that said *caring about the games is uncool* instead and gain a superior position that way. The cost performance of that option was much better. And that's why she didn't make an effort. From that perspective, I could put the principles behind Erika Konno's actions into simple words.

She was fulfilling her desire to save face by using her effort efficiently.

That formula included some speculation on my part, but I suspected it wasn't far off the mark. I'd taken information from Izumi, Gumi-chan, and Kikuchi-san, and assembled it the best I could to put Erika Konno's principles for action into words.

"...Okay, got it," I muttered, softly enough so only I could hear.

I hadn't been able to figure it out alone, but by gathering some missing information, I'd arrived at a conclusion of sorts. Before, I didn't even know what I should be aiming for. Now a goal had come into view.

If Erika Konno had manipulated the mood so that she could avoid putting any effort into the sports tournament—then all I had to do was somehow alter that mood. In other words, in order to take down the dragon, Erika Konno...

...I needed an item to make Erika Konno believe she'd lose face if our class didn't win the sports tournament.

By striking at the boss's weakness, I could provide the key to completing my assignment. Of course, I had no idea where to *find* that item, or whether there was some magic spell or weapon that could produce the same results. But if I knew the conditions I needed to fulfill, my general direction would become clear.

I'd collected information about this distinctive, normally unbeatable boss and finally discovered her weakness. Now to search for the key item that would get at that weakness!

Yeah, now that I was putting in some real effort, it was becoming clear. This game can be really fun sometimes.

Suddenly returning to Earth from my own little world, I met Kikuchi-san's eyes with my own, and she was smiling at me like she was watching over a child.

"Tomozaki-kun, you seem to be enjoying yourself."

"Uh...I—I do?"

Probably because I was thinking about games. Kikuchi-san laughed teasingly, but the sound was also genuinely happy.

"It's very you."

"Um, uh-huh..."

I was getting shy again—she always made me feel completely accepted.

* * *

After that, Kikuchi-san and I chatted calmly and quietly about Andi books, what we did over summer vacation, the kids in our class, and our plans after high school. It felt very natural to me, not talking about anything we didn't want to talk about and not having to wear masks in front of each other. When it was about time for us to leave, Kikuchi-san let something slip.

"I...should try harder, too."

"Huh? How so?" I asked. She smiled teasingly.

"Not that much time has passed since the day we went to buy books together, but...you've already changed so much."

Her smile looked warmer than usual, and her reply seemed more... girlish, somehow.

"H-have I really?"

Around two weeks had passed since that day. And from her perspective, I seemed different?

She nodded slowly.

"I think…you're facing the future more straightforwardly than you were before."

I thought back to what had happened with Hinami. Maybe Kikuchi-san was right—I had changed.

"…Huh."

Kikuchi-san's words touched something deep in my heart. I understood what she meant, and I realized she had the power to see through people. Quietly, she placed her supple, white, delicate palm on her chest.

"So…I'm going to try to do the same. A little at a time," she declared.

"…Yeah."

I didn't know where she wanted to go, or how she planned to get there. But if she'd made up her mind to start on a journey, then I wanted to be there to help her.

3

After a difficult quest, your latent abilities rise to the surface

That Monday, I was in Sewing Room #2.

"So have you made any progress on your assignment?"

As usual, I could hardly tell that Hinami had just finished morning practice. I decided to start with a basic overview of my current position.

"Um, well, I've finally got an idea of the conditions I need to create."

Hinami nodded admiringly.

"Wow. If you really have, you're moving faster than I expected."

"Really?"

I guess talking to all those people had sped up my progress.

"We still have plenty of time, so I'm not gonna ask you about your approach just yet. I'm looking forward to the outcome."

"You don't want to hear the details?"

"Nope. In the early stages of this assignment, you need to experiment for yourself."

As I suspected, it was on me to choose and implement a course of action independently instead of relying on Hinami's instructions.

"So you're telling me to stand on my own two feet?"

"Yup," she said curtly. The ideas behind this assignment were obvious from the way she was acting.

"Got it… By the way, I've been getting advice from a lot of people on how to tackle this. Do you have a problem with that?"

Hinami smiled and shook her head.

"No, that's actually the right approach. Isn't that what you typically do in games? Since you're up against a tough boss this time, you need to get help from other people on anything you can't handle alone. Making sure that's taken care of is part of the assignment."

"So this is good?"

"Yes."

"...Okay, got it."

I thought back to how I'd relied so heavily on Tama-chan when Mimimi needed help. This was similar. It was okay to get help from other people if I had a strategy but not the skills to carry it out on my own.

"But if you leave everything, including the planning, up to other people, then you've got your priorities backward. You're the one who needs to be playing the game. If you hand the controller over to someone else, there's no point to any of it. You understand that, right?"

"Yes, of course."

Having checked the rules with Hinami, I started planning my strategy.

* * *

We finished up the morning meeting and left Sewing Room #2. As soon as I got to our classroom, I noticed something. I walked over to Mizusawa and Takei.

"Nakamura...isn't coming today, either?"

Mizusawa frowned worriedly. "Seems that way. I sent him a message on LINE, but this is all I got back."

He showed me the conversation on his phone.

[*You skipping again? Something happen with Yoshiko?*
It's crazy how tough she is on you.
C'mon, don't ignore me.
Playing Dogfight *again?*]
[*Yeah.*
Tell Kawamura-sensei I have a fever.]

"Huh."

He was so damn stubborn. He ignored everything else and just made his point.

Dogfight was the game we were playing the other day at the arcade. So he was playing that again. Must be busy with both *Atafami* and *Dogfight* to keep up with. Well, for a gamer, that's not a bad thing.

"You see how he's acting? All I can do is leave him alone for a while."

Mizusawa sounded tired.

Takei agreed. "Shuji's so annoying when he gets like this!"

"S-so that's what's going on…"

I tried to judge how involved they were with the problem based on how they were reacting.

Mizusawa nodded. "This fight is really dragging on. He skipped school last Friday, and now he's skipping again after the weekend."

"Oh, has that not happened before?"

He nodded again. "Before, he'd typically take a day or so off, then come back to school like nothing happened… If they've been fighting all weekend, this could be their biggest blowup yet."

"Could be. Wonder what set 'em off this time," Takei said.

"No idea. I'll ask him later. Not that he'll answer me."

"All we can do is wait it out, huh?"

"Yeah. He better come back before the sports tournament, though. We're gonna need him."

"Geez, Takahiro. Now we know what *you* care about."

"Ha-ha-ha."

They wrapped up the conversation and shifted smoothly back to normal subjects. Listening to them talk, I noticed they were concerned about Nakamura, but they kept a certain distance. This must be how guy friendships work. I was stepping into a whole new world here.

The next morning, I was in class again before first period.

"Looks like he's breaking his record for longest absence," Mizusawa said, frowning.

Once again, Nakamura wasn't here. Even I was getting slightly worried.

I'd gotten used to my daily morning meeting with Mizusawa and Takei, but today, the mood was a little heavier than usual.

"He's taking it too far this time."

Takei was acting more or less the same as always, but I sensed anxiety now. I didn't know he was capable of that emotion.

"I got this from him," Mizusawa said, showing us his phone.

[*Say I've had a fever all week.*]

My mouth dropped open.

"This is getting worse."

Mizusawa nodded.

"Yeah. I mean, we have exams coming up. We're about to start prepping for them, and it's gonna hit hard if he misses the whole first part."

"...True."

I agreed. The teachers were handing out worksheets and booklets and explaining how to use them and how their classes would generally go. If he missed all that, it wouldn't be a fatal blow, but it definitely wouldn't be good.

"Shit. What the hell is he thinking?!"

Takei ran his fingers through his hair, genuinely upset. Mizusawa smiled slightly as he watched him, but his eyes were serious.

"Well, he might know all this already, but Shuji never liked thinking things through."

Mizusawa scratched his neck, then folded his arms in thought.

First period ended after a painful initiation into math, and then we had a short break. Suddenly, I felt someone poking my left shoulder.

"Ack!"

"Overreaction much?"

I looked to my left and saw Izumi leaning away from me with a frown.

"Oh, s-sorry."

I might have gotten somewhat used to talking to and even teasing people lately, but I still fell apart when someone caught me off guard. I'm still a bottom-tier character, after all.

"What's up?" I asked. Izumi glanced down but then made eye contact.

"I was just…wondering about Shuji."

She looked very serious, and her cheeks were slightly flushed. Now this was a top-tier character—stirring my protective instincts with her vulnerability. Crafty, too. But I knew how these top-tier characters used their cuteness, and I stayed firm.

"Uh…um, you mean about him being absent?"

When I finally managed a response, I found I was more shaken than I thought, but it wasn't a big deal. Izumi was as flustered as usual to be talking about Nakamura.

"Yeah," she said with a nod. "I saw you talking to Hiro a minute ago, so I thought you might know something."

Oh right, Izumi called Mizusawa "Hiro." I wasn't sure how to respond.

"…Well, on the one hand, he's just skipping today, but we were saying he's gonna have a hard time if this keeps up."

"Yeah, that's what I was thinking," she said, nodding glumly. "Wonder how long this'll go on."

I thought back to the LINE message Mizusawa had shown me.

"Mizusawa got a message saying he'd be out all week."

"From Shuji?"

"Yeah."

"All week? Yikes."

I agreed. "Yeah. We've got entrance exams to think about, and if he misses the beginning of the exam-prep classes, he'll be in a bad place."

"Oh…I hadn't even thought of that."

Izumi seemed to be uncertain about something. I wondered what exactly she meant.

"What were you thinking about?"

"Oh, nothing… It's just…"

Izumi paused, scratching her nose, before continuing. "It seems like he fights with his parents a lot, but it's already been a week. And it's still not over. Like, missing school is bad, too, but…I'm worried about his relationship with his parents."

"Oh…"

I hadn't thought that deeply about the situation. I already knew Izumi had a kind heart, but seeing her worry about Nakamura's relationship with his mom was another reminder. She really had a lot of empathy for him.

"That's important, too, right?" she said.

"Yeah."

Izumi bit her lip worriedly. "If he would at least come to school, I could drag the whole story out of him. But if he's not here, there's nothing I can do..."

She sighed with exasperation, and I decided to bring up the point Mizusawa and Takei had been talking about the day before.

"He'll come in time for the sports tournament...won't he?"

"Maybe? I hope he does. If we're going to do it, I'd rather everyone be there."

"Me too..."

"Yeah." Izumi nodded solemnly.

"We were just talking about how he tends to act before he thinks."

"Oh, he totally does," she said, pointing at me. Guess I hit the nail on the head.

I couldn't help but smile ruefully. "So he's always like that, huh?"

Izumi knew that about him, and she liked him anyway. When you're in love, everything about the other person is beautiful to you, huh? Aww.

"That's just who he is. We were in the same class last year, so I'm used to it."

She sounded happily resigned to his flaws.

"You sound like you're already married!" I joked.

Izumi turned red. *How about that? That was actually kinda smooth, wasn't it?* It came out so naturally because I wasn't really trying—I just said what I thought, and it happened to have that result. I felt like I'd been button mashing and accidentally delivered a perfect uppercut. Oh well—it worked out just fine, looks like.

* * *

It was sixth period, the last class of the day—a long homeroom.

"All right, since we chose the captains for the sports tournament last week, let's nail down a few other things for the tournament today," Kawamura-sensei said, writing the words *Top Sports Choices* on the board. We were starting the meeting without Nakamura. "Like last year, the boys and girls in each grade level will choose one sport respectively and compete against the other classes in the same grade. Last year, we had...soccer, basketball, dodgeball, volleyball, and softball. But as long as a court is open, you can choose other sports, too. Captains, please lead the discussion... Takei, Hirabayashi, come up here."

She gestured for the two of them to come to the front of the class.

"All right, guys! We're going with soccer, right?!"

The class giggled as Takei walked up to the front. Hirabayashi-san followed quietly in his shadow. She didn't seem used to this kind of role. All I could do was let Takei handle the situation. *I don't quite trust you, man, but...do your best to take the lead, okay?*

"There's no guarantee you'll get your first choice at the captains' meetings, so you should choose your top three. I've heard Takei always loses at rock-paper-scissors, so that's the safest bet."

"Hey! C'mon, you're supposed to be a teacher!"

The class laughed again. When I looked at Hirabayashi-san, I could see she was too nervous to fully smile, but at least she looked amused. *Keep it up, Takei.*

I glanced at Erika Konno. She was laughing normally. Maybe she didn't need to be uptight now that the captains had been chosen. At moments like this, she reminded me of one of those trendsetting fashionistas—cute and impossible to ignore. Her ordinary attitude was just too scary.

Anyway, sports. And motivating Erika Konno. We had to make the right choice here if I was going to complete my assignment. If our first choice ended up being something she hated, the cost part of the cost-performance equation would go up.

"...Hey, Izumi," I whispered. After all, we had the same goal here. "Which sport do you think Konno would care about the most?"

"Hmm..." She whispered back, "Maybe softball?"

"Huh. Really?"

I'd been expecting her to say *none*, so a straightforward answer like this was good news.

"Yeah… She doesn't wanna get hit with a ball, so dodgeball, volleyball, soccer, and basketball are out."

"Oh, makes sense…" That was one way to narrow it down. "Does she like any other sports?"

"Let's see… She's fairly athletic, but I haven't really seen her having fun with anything else."

"Huh…"

"I think we should try to get everyone on board with softball."

"Okay."

I nodded. Izumi took a deep breath, preparing herself for a fight. I liked that gamer spirit—figure out what you need to do and do it. *Nice job, apprentice! I better give this my all, too.* Not that I had much say in which sport the girls chose.

"Okay, you have twenty minutes, guys. Until…two thirty-five. Captains, you're in charge of the discussion. The best option is to come to a consensus. If you can't, we'll decide by majority rule. We'll start with the boys."

"We're going with soccer, right?!"

The second Kawamura-sensei handed the reins to Takei, he made his proposal to the class. This wasn't so much a normie thing as it was just…a Takei thing. He'd announced soccer as his choice as soon as he got the position, so I didn't expect much discussion.

I was wrong.

"Nah, we should do basketball!"

Tachibana, the guy I'd talked to the other day, was rebelling. Before, I'd only guessed he was on the basketball team, but it looked like I was right. I hadn't expected the guys to split at this point in the process. I'd better observe and analyze the situation carefully to figure out why.

"What?! You're kidding! Not soccer?!" Takei said, throwing the "leader" mantle out the window. Typical Takei.

"I'd rather do softball."

The second guy to shoot his arrow was a member of Tachibana's group.

Uh, what was his name? Shimizudani? He was buff and had a shaved head, which suggested he was on the baseball team. I think I've been judging people based on their looks too much lately.

"Okay, softball is fun, but..."

Once again, Takei wasn't so much pulling the class together as saying his personal opinion. *Yeah, you're not really suited for this.* I thought about why the class hadn't just gone along with soccer, even though Takei had announced before that he would get us soccer in the captains' meeting. Plus, the high-ranking Nakamura was on the soccer team. Then it hit me.

Nakamura wasn't here.

The guys who'd just suggested basketball and softball were jocks—they had decent status, but they were below Nakamura. They had less power in the class even though they had more members in their group.

If Nakamura had been here, the midranking guys would probably have gone along with whatever he wanted, but since he wasn't around to control the mood, some individuals had started to splinter off, dividing the overall opinion. It was starting to come together. And since there were so many of them, we could be in big trouble. Wow, Nakamura has a huge presence, doesn't he?

"We've got a lot of guys on the basketball team, so we could probably win."

"True!"

"We've got a lot on the baseball team, too..."

"Yeah, both could work."

Multiple positions were emerging within the jock group. They weren't being pushy, though. It was more like they were testing the waters and adjusting in response to one another. Compared with Nakamura's usual method of insisting on what he wanted, these guys seemed downright considerate. Their group probably had no clear central figure equivalent to Nakamura, and so they had no clear, single direction.

Takei looked helpless. He was probably panicking because he couldn't get everyone to reach a consensus.

"Uh, so what are we going with? Soccer, basketball, and softball?" he asked.

"I say we just vote."

"Yeah, sounds good," Takei said, nodding. We were going to vote before the time limit was even up. Takei wrote *Soccer, Basketball,* and *Softball* on the board and started to count up votes.

"Okay, guys, who votes for soccer?"

Aside from Takei, only three other guys raised their hand, including Mizusawa. I didn't raise my hand, by the way. I might suck at sports, but I planned to vote for basketball to get at least some enjoyment out of this event. For us nerds, manipulating a ball with our feet or a bat is even harder than throwing it. *Sorry, Takei, I've gotta vote for fun. Sorry to you, too, Nakamura.*

"Seriously?" Takei sighed, writing a big *4* next to *Soccer.* Uh, I think people usually use tally marks for stuff like this. I almost laughed, just because it was such a Takei thing to do. Close call.

He took the votes for basketball and softball and ended up with nine for the former and six for the latter, which decided the ranking of our top three choices. Soccer was third, unbelievably. With Nakamura out, the midlevel guys had fragmented, and then all the lower-ranking "boring" guys in the class had gone for basketball. They probably figured they could get away without much court time—I know, because that's how I thought until this year.

"Shit, no way! It's basketball, then softball, then soccer."

Takei wasn't even pretending to be neutral about this. The guys' discussion was over in around five minutes, and the baton was passed to Hirabayashi-san.

"Um, so let's decide on the girls' top choices now."

The class suddenly felt very quiet. It was probably because Takei was so loud, but as everyone sensed the hush, the whole temperature of the class grew colder and colder. I glanced around, observing the people sitting nearby. They all looked tense. Or maybe I was just making assumptions.

I looked at Erika Konno, wondering what she would do in this situation. I watched as she slowly removed her hand from her cheek, folded her arms over her chest, and slumped grumpily back in her chair. Well, that was easy to read. Just watching her or sitting near her would be enough to make you shrink in on yourself a little.

"...Damn," Izumi whispered.

"...Erika Konno?" I whispered back. She nodded rapidly several times, her round eyes glittering. She reminded me of a frightened dog. But yeah, given how obvious Erika Konno was making her opinion, everyone must have noticed it. That's when I realized something.

Was this another method Erika Konno used to control the mood?

She displayed her opinion not just with words, but with her glances, posture, and actions. In fact, the first thing Hinami taught me was how to control my own expression and posture.

Thanks to her, I could tell a healthy debate would be hard, but that didn't mean the class had completely frozen up.

"I vote for basketball! With Hinami and me on the team, we'll win for sure!" Mimimi was waving her hand enthusiastically.

"Well, I can probably only be there for half the game," Hinami said, smiling a little regretfully.

"What?! ...Oh right. You're student council president!"

"Yup. But I still think basketball is best."

They were cheerfully ignoring Erika Konno and carrying out their own plans. Unlike the guys, who were dominated by Nakamura's group, the girls in class had two major factions: the Konno group and the Hinami group. There was more to the power structure than met the eye.

"Okay, basketball... Anyone else?"

No one responded to Hirabayashi-san's question. Shit. Someone needed to do something, or we'd never end up with softball. I checked to see how Izumi was doing. She seemed nervous, too, glancing back and forth between Mimimi, Hinami, and Hirabayashi-san. Finally, she looked at me. I nodded rapidly a few times to encourage her. *Damn, I'm picking up more of her gestures.* She nodded back at me a couple times herself. After a few more moments of hesitation—

"I wanna do volleyball," Tama-chan said, shooting her hand straight up. *Huh?* Izumi's hand was already halfway in the air; she brought it to her head and combed her hair with her fingers instead. *Come on, don't wimp out!* Of course, I knew where she was coming from.

"Okay, volleyball. What should we do? Which one should be our first choice? Or does anyone else have a suggestion?"

Rather than rushing into the majority rule like Takei, Hirabayashi-san was trying to follow Kawamura-sensei's instructions to decide by consensus. Good job.

Tama-chan had some real power in situations like this. The queen at the top of the hierarchy had created a silence so heavy, only Hinami and Mimimi could break it, and yet Tama-chan still raised a third opinion. Maybe it was because she was friends with those two. Either way, it was impressive.

It seemed likely to end up a close call between basketball or volleyball. Izumi glanced at me again uncertainly. Of course she was nervous. Suggesting yet another choice at this point would take some willpower. That was understandable. From the outside, it didn't seem like much, but when you were the one sticking your neck out, it was exhausting.

Still, setting the stage properly was crucial if we were going to convince the queen. Plus, it would be way easier to have fun in the tournament and help Hirabayashi-san if both of the top two girls' cliques in class were on board. I pumped my fist at Izumi to encourage her some more. She nodded rapidly again like a dog and turned decisively toward the front.

"...I think I'd rather do softball," she said, timidly raising her hand. *Yes! You did it, Izumi!*

"Okay, softball. Um, do each of you have a reason for your choice? Oh, Nanami-san already said why she wanted basketball," Hirabayashi-san said. She sounded hesitant, but she was sticking with the consensus method. "Natsubayashi-san, how about you?"

Tama-chan paused for a moment.

"Uh...because I want to play volleyball?"

There was a brief, awkward silence. Maybe a little too honest.

"Come on, that's not a real reason!" Mimimi shot back jokingly, gesturing comically with both arms outstretched. That was the signal for the class to burst into laughter. *Okay, so this is another method for getting the group to laugh—poke fun at someone else if they say something a little weird.* I tried to imagine myself doing that at some future point. Key word being *tried.* Yeah, that was still beyond me, even on an imaginary level.

In any case, that was an impressive move by Mimimi. Not only did she make the group laugh, but she was protecting Tama-chan. I remembered that Tama-chan had been described as not very flexible. In the exchange just now, Mimimi had very clearly helped her blend into the group. If she hadn't done anything, we might still be in an awkward silence.

"Okay, Izumi-san, you're next…"

Just as we were about to continue the discussion, a grumpy voice interrupted.

"Look, if we can't all agree, we should just vote."

The queen was attacking the captain.

"Uh, um, yes, but…"

Hirabayashi-san immediately crumbled before the intimidating and vaguely hostile reply. She glanced at Kawamura-sensei and the rest of us pleadingly, and the teacher finally stepped in.

"…Konno. I'd rather not jump straight to using the majority rule. I was hoping we could try coming to an agreement through dialogue. So I'm going to take over from here. Okay, first…"

With that, she smoothly took over leading the discussion, protecting Hirabayashi-san with cool confidence. Hirabayashi-san sighed with relief.

Pretty soon, Izumi-san was giving her reason for choosing softball, which was carefully adjusted to fit the general mood. I glanced at Erika Konno. Like before, she was leaning back in her chair with her legs crossed to make sure we all knew she was bored. Izumi sat back down. Our eyes met.

"…Erika scared me to death," she whispered.

"Yeah…," I whispered back as I kept watching the discussion.

Ultimately, the girls took a vote: six for basketball, five for softball, and two for volleyball. That made basketball their first choice. Welp. So much for softball. Guess this wouldn't be so easy.

To be honest, I hadn't expected Erika Konno to vote at all, but Kawamura-sensei was watching her. She ended up voting for softball, so Izumi had been right. She really was good at reading people.

After the discussion, we had a break. Izumi was slumped on her desk, looking exhausted.

"…Nice work."

I wanted to congratulate her for surviving, even if it was a small struggle in the scope of things. She looked up at me and smiled vulnerably.

"Thanks."

"Of course."

Her unguarded face was like a magnet drawing my eyes. I forced myself to look away so I could regain my composure, and thought about our next move.

"Konno is an iron wall, isn't she…? I can't imagine her getting into this."

"Ah-ha-ha, me neither."

She smiled naively, trustingly. *Stop that! If you don't, I might trust you, too.* Wait, is that really such a bad thing?

"At this rate, we're gonna have a hard time no matter what sport we get."

"Yeah. Maybe I should give up on this. But poor Hirabayashi-san…" Izumi sighed.

"We're going to need some new tactics…"

Izumi looked at me blankly.

"Tactics? Oh yeah, I guess so. Do you have any ideas?"

"N-not yet…" Tactics—something to hit her weak points. "I'll give it some thought."

"All right!" Izumi said, making an *okay* sign with her finger and thumb.

Hmm… So we needed a way to get Erika Konno excited. Some trick to convince her that everyone will look down on her if she doesn't. Or we could appeal to something else she wants.

I asked Izumi some more questions about Konno, but I didn't get any new information or new ideas. Still, I felt like I was on the verge of a breakthrough.

* * *

It was after school, and I was at my usual meeting—but not the one in Sewing Room #2. This time, I was standing at the window where Nakamura's group always hung out.

Mizusawa, Takei, and I had been chatting when Izumi and Hinami joined the conversation, which eventually turned to the Nakamura issue. Apparently, all the sports teams and clubs had the day off because the teachers were at some training event away from school. It went without saying that the topic of conversation was whether or not we should leave Nakamura alone.

"...I mean, there's not much we can do," Mizusawa said.

Hinami smiled cynically. "Yeah, it's tough when he won't tell us what's going on."

"Exactly," Izumi said, nodding.

Mizusawa frowned. "Which means...we really shouldn't do anything. At least for now."

Izumi seemed upset by this idea. "What? Why? If there's something we can do, we should do it, right?"

Takei nodded. "I think Yuzucchi is right! If Nakamura's in trouble, we've gotta help him!"

"Okay, but...," Hinami said with a vaguely reluctant smile, "it *is* a family issue, and Shuji doesn't seem to want us to get involved..."

"And that's our real problem," Mizusawa said.

They were right. I understood Izumi's and Takei's desire to help, but it was a delicate question. How far do you stick your nose into a family fight? Hinami nodded at Mizusawa with a frustrated look on her face.

"Yeah. If we force our way in when he doesn't want us involved, we'd just end up being pushy..."

The group was silent for a moment. I wasn't sure if Hinami's comment came from the heroine mask or NO NAME, logic incarnate, but I got the sense it reflected her true feelings. I mean, this was directly related to her earlier point about rights and responsibility.

"Your rights only extend as far as you can take responsibility."

Imagine if we butted into Nakamura's problem without his permission, and something bad ended up happening. None of us would be ready for that level of responsibility. Ergo, we shouldn't get involved. Personally, I agreed.

"I guess so...," Izumi finally said. She seemed convinced, but unsure what to do.

"Yeah, Takahiro and Aoi are usually right, but still..."

Takei also sounded uncertain, even though he was putting his trust in the other two.

"We can let him know we're here for him if he needs to talk, but I really think we should hold off on anything else," Hinami urged.

"Yeah...you're right."

Izumi was clearly depressed, but she nodded slowly. She probably still wanted to help, but Hinami believed that acting on one's own desires was the wrong choice in this case. She was wearing her perfect heroine mask and softening the edges of her words, but she was still trying to control Izumi.

A quiet disagreement was taking place.

Hinami's unwavering principle was to choose the most rational path of action. It was extreme, but it had put her at the top in all realms of life, so of course she was going to keep Izumi, who just wanted to do something different, from acting irrationally. But then a thought occurred to me.

I'm not Hinami.

I have one basic guiding principle: I plan to enjoy the game of life, so I put what I want first. Meaning, I shouldn't just choose the most rational approach like Hinami did. If I was really trying to live life consciously, I needed to ask myself what *I* wanted in this situation. Answering that question was my first order of business.

"..."

Not that I was any good at it yet, but I tried to sort out my emotions into words. I needed to prioritize my own feelings, my own direction, my own wants.

For a moment, I remained introspective, groping for an answer. Then I looked at the dejected face of my apprentice, Izumi, and made my decision.

It was very different from Hinami's "rational" conclusion, but I felt like I had to stick with it. And if I wanted to make it happen, I'd need to get the mood on my side. I came up with a plan, carefully chose my words, and turned to the group.

"I agree; we shouldn't get involved in Nakamura's problems carelessly."

Basically, the current situation called for waiting it out. Hinami was right that the logical way to handle this was to wait until he came to us for help. And that was why I kept talking.

"...But here's the thing."

"...Hmm?"

It was Hinami, not Izumi, who reacted. I kept going, in part to organize my own thoughts and in part to make them into reality.

"It *would* be a mistake to do something before he asks. But I think we can start getting ready now to help him when he does."

"...How?" Hinami sounded unconvinced.

"Yeah, what do you mean?"

Izumi's eyes glittered with a small spark of hope. I continued explaining my idea to the two of them.

"It would be wrong to, like, force him back to school or say something to his mom so they make up. But as long as we don't make things worse, I think it would be a good idea to try to find out what's going on and start getting ready to help him in case we do need to act eventually. We wouldn't implement any plans just yet, but we'd be prepared to help when he needs it."

I wasn't saying anything groundbreaking—just that we could start thinking about this now. Maybe he'd never ask us and we were wasting our time, but what I wanted in this situation was extremely simple.

I wanted to respect Izumi's desire to help Nakamura.

That was the conclusion I'd come to after taking a look into my own heart.

"Yeah, yeah! Maybe we could end up helping him!"

"Exactly," I said, nodding at the sparkly-eyed Izumi. I glanced quickly at Hinami, then back at Izumi. "If you want to help him, then I think you should go for it and give it your all."

I was talking to Izumi, but I was also sending a little irony Hinami's way. What can I say? It's how I really felt.

"Yeah! I totally get you," Izumi said excitedly.

"Huh… I guess that's one way to look at it."

Hinami looked unsure, but on the surface, at least, she wasn't contradicting me. After all, I wasn't saying anything that extreme. I was only suggesting we do everything we could, regardless of whether it'd end up being a waste of time. She probably couldn't find a reason good enough for the perfect heroine Aoi Hinami to contradict that idea.

But I could read her real thoughts like a book.

Right now, Nakamura was rejecting any involvement from us. And knowing him, he wasn't gonna change his mind. Anything we did now was almost certainly going to be a waste of time, and that wouldn't accomplish her goals. It would be ineffective, unproductive, and just not an objectively good decision. If we had time for this, we'd be better off using it for something productive. Therefore, we should take a wait-and-see approach.

Taking it even further, if Nakamura had chosen a course of action that would cause himself harm, he should take responsibility for his own decisions. There was no need for us to go out of our way to help him.

I would have bet money that was what she was thinking. I'm a gamer, too; I get it. And I essentially agreed with her.

But life was just more *fun* when you put what you wanted first. That was my philosophy.

I'd told Hinami I would teach her how to enjoy life, and I meant it. We were starting now. I had no idea if it was the "correct" thing to do, but we shouldn't set the bar too high just yet!

"Let's give it a try!"

Izumi looked around at everyone with her innocent eyes. She wanted to help so badly; she really was in love. In my opinion, that's one of the hardest "moods" in the whole world to overturn. So this time, I was using it to my advantage. I figured it wouldn't be a bad thing if the mood respected what Izumi wanted. Maybe I had inherited some of Hinami's cold logic. The important point was that the goal itself wasn't false.

"Fine, if Fumiya insists, I guess we can try it out," Mizusawa said, smiling with exasperation.

"Yeah!" Izumi said brightly.

Takei nodded, too. "I'm with Farm Boy!" he said.

Once we'd established that, even Aoi Hinami would have a hard time reversing the course. I grinned and looked at her. For just an instant, she met my eyes with a meaningful glare.

"Agreed! It definitely makes sense to give it a try!" she said with the smile of a perfect heroine. As usual, an impeccable performance. I knew she was internally groaning about the waste of time, but she couldn't say that without breaking character. Her mask had come back to bite her. She had to accept a truly irrational plan so that Izumi and I could get what we wanted.

"All right, so we'll do what we can."

As Mizusawa restated the final decision, our overall direction fell into place. Hinami looked at us nonchalantly.

"So the first thing we need to do..."

She took the lead in organizing our plan. Wow. Slightly surprising, yet in character. Even if the direction wasn't what she'd hoped for, once it was decided, she'd throw herself into making it as efficient as possible. She'd never allow these irrational standards to take hold. That defiance was her strength.

Oh, and if she asks me later why I suggested that plan, I'm going to tell her I thought it would be good experience for defeating Erika Konno. That should save me. Making excuses is an important life skill.

* * *

The discussion began, with Hinami at the center.

"First of all, if we don't know what's going on with Shuji, we can't do much to help. I think we have two options to learn why he's been gone for so long—we either find a subtle way of asking him directly, or we ask his mom without making everything worse."

Mizusawa turned to her in surprise.

"Wouldn't asking his mom be a little much? Just going to his house would be making a huge deal out of it."

Hinami shook her head.

"Well...he's got a lot of handouts on his desk now, right?"

"Huh? Oh yeah," Mizusawa said, nodding but still confused.

"Plus, he texted you saying he wouldn't be back for another week, right? We could say you offered to bring them home to him when you told the teacher. Like, *If he's going to miss a whole week, we thought we'd come by!*"

"Oh...yeah, I guess that wouldn't be weird." Mizusawa sounded a bit outmaneuvered.

"And since he's still fighting with his mom, he won't be home. Then we can just strike up a conversation! If we're smart about it, we should be able to find out why they're fighting! But we don't want to make too big a deal out of it, so we should probably only have one person go. She may be a tough nut to crack...but I think I can handle it!"

Hinami jokingly made a macho muscleman pose with one arm. I was honestly surprised by how smoothly she explained her ideas while keeping the whole mood positive. I'd intended to pull her into a more subjective approach, but instead she'd created a pocket of rationality within this irrationality and was racing along the shortest path possible to a solution.

I realized I'd never actually seen her work at solving a problem. She was always the one putting me through tests, so she didn't offer solutions herself. I'd like to steal a few skills from this girl. After all, observation was one of my assignments, wasn't it?

As I watched her speedily string together the most relevant bits of information we currently had and casually propose a workable plan, I felt like I was witnessing the very essence of Aoi Hinami, a terrifying force of efficiency and productivity. If this plan failed, she'd have two or three more waiting in the wings.

"Makes sense to me...so can we leave it to you, Aoi?"

Mizusawa was once again attempting to pull together the group's position when someone interrupted.

* * *

"Um, would it be bad if I was the one to do it?"

It was Izumi—shy but resolute.

"Uhhh..."

Hinami hesitated. What was she thinking right now? She was probably searching for a way to turn down Izumi's suggestion without causing trouble. Or maybe she was calculating the risk of failure that would come with handing off the job. Before she could say anything else, though, Izumi broke in again, more forcefully this time.

"I *want* to do it."

She looked at Hinami with even more determination than before. I'd never seen her fight this hard against her tendency to disappear into the flow. Ah, the power of love.

I was fairly sure she was taking this stand because she wanted to help Nakamura personally. It wasn't a rational position. She was just putting her feelings out there. The power of her will to do what she wanted was no joke, but it had no logic to back it up.

Basically, this was about as irrational as you could get. She was totally prioritizing her own desires over efficient problem-solving. Of course Hinami disapproved.

"I totally get where you're coming from, but..."

Her tone was bright, but she avoided saying anything conclusive. Just as she was trying to find the shortest possible path of escape from an illogical approach, Izumi was again blocking her way.

Izumi's proposal might have been irrational, but it arose straight out of her very genuine feelings for Nakamura. The perfect heroine couldn't very well toss the idea away without a backward glance. Hinami was probably internally screaming. This was getting fun. The mood of the maiden in love was powerful indeed.

Eventually, Hinami broke her silence.

"Okay! It's in your hands, Yuzu!"

Once again, logic had lost. She probably had to accept irrational choices now and then as part of her role as the perfect heroine, but doing

so when she had to solve a practical problem was the polar opposite of Aoi Hinami's approach to life.

Takei jumped in with a joke.

"You sure you can handle this, Yuzucchi?! Don't you think you should leave it to Aoi?!"

I was surprised to hear Takei using his head, even accidentally, but Izumi just raised one finger and winked.

"Leave it to me! I'm an expert at reading a room!"

She looked at me and smiled. Why was she being so masochistic? And looking at me? Was it because she'd talked to me about this? Well, if she was comfortable enough to poke fun at it, that was a good thing. Plus, she was doing a good job of stating her opinion.

In this short period of time, she'd really made progress. EXP gained from love was a marvel to behold. Leveling up in life wasn't exactly a competition, but I couldn't let my guard down with her.

"Gotcha. So that's the plan," Mizusawa said, wrapping up the meeting.

"All right, step one: talking to Kawamura-sensei!" cried Hinami.

With that, the plan swung into action.

* * *

About an hour later, after Kawamura-sensei gave the go-ahead and Mizusawa led us to Nakamura's house, Izumi headed off to her task while the rest of us went to wait in front of a convenience store nearby. We'd been there for about fifteen minutes when Hinami started to worry.

"It's been a while..."

Takei nodded.

"I wonder what they're talking about."

"Maybe Shuji was home, and they got into a conversation," said Mizusawa.

We hung out, chatting and making random guesses, for another ten minutes or so. Finally, Izumi returned, and she looked exhausted.

"Hey! What were you doing in there, Yuzucchi?!" Takei asked, waving exaggeratedly. Izumi waved weakly back, holding her hand at chest level.

"I got the info… Had to listen to Shuji's mom complain about him the whole time…"

She gave a thin, weak laugh.

"Good work…," I said, almost without thinking.

"Yeah…thanks."

Izumi rested both her arms on Hinami's shoulder and slumped there. Hinami patted her head.

"There, there."

"I'm not a baby!" Izumi protested. Hinami kept patting her head for a little too long, teasing her. This was fun to watch.

After a minute, Izumi leaped away from Hinami and clapped her hands.

"…Anyway!"

"So? Why are they fighting?" Hinami asked, smoothly switching modes. Izumi nodded quickly.

"I figured it out! Well, I mean, she just kind of told me, but…"

She smiled awkwardly.

"…C'mon, tell us!" Hinami said eagerly, watching her.

Izumi sighed and frowned as she answered.

"He was playing *Atafami* too much, so she told him he couldn't play at home anymore. That's why they got in a huge fight…"

…

Everyone was silent for a second. Then Mizusawa and Takei both let out huge sighs.

"I think I've finally met someone dumber than Takei…"

"Hey! Wait a second, that's harsh!"

Izumi sighed, too, watching them. I could tell she thought it was about the stupidest reason ever for such a big fight.

But I also had my own feelings about this, and I probably wasn't the only one. I glanced at Hinami. She was looking at me. We nodded at each other, confirming our unspoken thought, then looked away. When we heard the reason for Nakamura's fight, we'd been on the same wavelength.

* * *

I don't care what's going on; you can't just ban Atafami*!*

But I decided not to let it show.

* * *

After leaving the convenience store, we went to a family restaurant nearby.

"Well, whatever his reason, now is not a good time to be missing a lot of school..."

Our morale had plunged, and Mizusawa was trying to boost it again by reminding us of our goal.

"Yeah. It's really not. Anyway, the reason may be dumb, but a fight's a fight...," Izumi said weakly, like she was trying to find her motivation again.

"Right..." Takei was completely deflated.

On the other hand, Hinami and I were both feeling a little more motivated than before.

"Yeah, we can't let it stay like this forever."

"Exactly! Plus, it must be tough not being allowed to do his favorite thing!"

"What's with you two...?" Mizusawa said, noticing the difference and looking at us suspiciously. Hinami quickly changed the subject.

"Anyway, I think there's a lot we can do!"

"Really?! Like what?!"

Izumi scooted up against her and waited eagerly for her next words.

"Shuji's mom probably thinks playing *Atafami* makes his brain rot or something."

"Oh... Yeah, she did seem to think that!"

"So...Tomozaki-kun," Hinami said, suddenly mentioning me by name.

"Huh?"

"What was your class ranking at the end of last semester?"

"Um, last semester? Around fortieth..."

Actually, it was thirty-eighth. Given there were a little under two hundred kids in our year, that wasn't bad. I didn't have bottom-tier grades, at least. But why was she asking?

"So you're probably above Shuji, right?"

Mizusawa nodded. "Yeah. He's not too bad, but I'm guessing he's right around the middle."

Hinami grinned. "Plus…I've actually been playing a lot of *Atafami* myself lately."

"Really? Guess everyone's getting into it these days." Mizusawa smiled.

She said "lately," but NO NAME popped up online more than six months ago. Well, in gamer terms, that was recent.

"Yup. Which means Tomozaki-kun and I both play *Atafami*, and both of us are fairly good students. What if we found a way to casually drop that info in front of Shuji's mom?"

"…Aha."

Mizusawa smiled, but without much enthusiasm.

I got Hinami's point, too. She continued happily.

"Couldn't we clear up her misconception that *Atafami* makes you dumb?"

The idea was slightly silly, but if the plan went well, the problem would be resolved almost instantly. Telling her we were both good students and *Atafami* players would be easy enough.

Mizusawa wasn't really enjoying this conversation, but he rubbed his chin solemnly.

"It's not a bad idea… From what I've heard about Yoshiko, she'd have respect for the top student in the class."

"…True."

I nodded. It was a stereotype, but I definitely had an image of those overzealous helicopter moms latching onto trustworthy information about other people: *The smartest kid in class is doing such and such!*

Plus, I might not be that convincing on my own with my grades, but the other *Atafami* player happened to be Aoi Hinami, who was at the top of the class. This boosted the persuasiveness of our argument significantly. We could even argue that *Atafami* was excellent exercise for the brain. The strategy was classic Hinami: a head-on attack; bulldozing through with sheer effort.

Mizusawa agreed.

"So basically, we'll have Aoi go and chat with Shuji's mom… But hasn't it been a while since last semester's exams? Wouldn't it be unnatural bringing them up now?"

Aoi acted unsure for a second. Right before she answered, her lips seemed to curl upward very briefly, but maybe it was just my imagination. I was still bracing for the worst.

"You have a point… It's already second semester, so that might be weird… Maybe something else would be more natural."

"Like what?" Mizusawa asked. Hinami hesitated again and then, for some reason, looked me in the eye as she continued.

"We have a math quiz the day after tomorrow, right?"

"Huh? Uh, yeah, but so what?" I had a bad feeling about this.

Hinami grinned. "Well, when we go to his house again in a few days to bring him his handouts…we'll bring Tomozaki-kun's and my answer sheets from the test! With scores of at least ninety."

"What?!"

Hinami's full-on sadism threw me for a loop. *Hold up! Ninety percent?!*

"M-math isn't my best subject…," I protested.

Hinami laughed. Though she was smiling, her eyes were glittering sadistically.

"Maybe so, but can't you try a little harder than usual for Shuji's sake?"

"Uh, okay…"

I was trapped; she was using the same argument I'd used earlier. What a perfect counter. She was getting her revenge.

"Uh, um…"

Suddenly, Izumi broke in, haltingly but with determination. I glanced at her, and she was timidly holding up her hand next to her face. Hinami blinked dramatically.

"Yes, Yuzu?"

Izumi looked at her.

"I've been playing *Atafami* lately, too."

"Oh, you have?"

I could tell Hinami wasn't ready for that.

Izumi nodded firmly. "Tomozaki told me I was almost ready to be Shuji's practice partner. I think I practice more than most people!"

"Really?" Hinami said, tilting her head quizzically. She didn't sound very convinced.

Eventually, Izumi's gaze stopped shifting around, and she met Hinami's eyes.

"So I'm thinking that if I also do well on the math quiz, maybe that'll help convince her, too."

She waited solemnly for Hinami's answer. Once again, she was insisting on what she wanted.

Hinami glanced at me, probably to see whether Izumi was telling the truth about *Atafami*. Or maybe she was thinking the two of us were enough, and Izumi didn't need to take the trouble to score high on the quiz. And Hinami would never recommend wasting effort. After all, between the famous Aoi Hinami and an extra person like me, we ought to be plenty convincing. Not to mention, she was just good at talking people into things.

From Hinami's logical perspective, Izumi didn't need to wear herself out trying to ace the quiz. Which was why I decided to argue.

"Izumi has been practicing hard lately, that's for sure. And I know what I'm talking about when it comes to *Atafami*. I think it's a good idea for her to join us."

Still looking at me, Hinami furrowed her brows for a second, then went back to smiling cheerfully. Well, she might have her ideas about what's best, but I'd made up my mind to respect Izumi's desire to help the boy she liked. Logic would just have to take a day off. After all, I knew what it felt like to want to achieve something. Really, *really* knew.

"...All right, then!"

Hinami clapped her hands, pushing the conversation along. Her tone was bright and sincere, but I bet she was complaining deep down. *"So that's your approach, huh, Tomozaki?"* I was gonna pay for this.

"So the three of us will get scores of at least ninety percent on our math quiz! And when we bring the quiz to Shuji, we'll casually bring it up during a conversation with his mom! Sound good?"

"Yeah!"

"Sure."

Izumi and I nodded, and so did Takei and Mizusawa. Hinami smiled enthusiastically. It was so weird how her smile could be so nice when this wasn't going her way at all.

"The only other thing is whether Shuji would actually want us to do it," she said.

"That's the question, isn't it?" Mizusawa smiled.

It wasn't like we were going to make things worse, but Nakamura probably wouldn't take very well to us going over and getting information from his mom, then coming back with a math quiz and making a little speech about how playing *Atafami* doesn't rot your brain or whatever. In which case, somebody should probably get him on board with our plan first…

"So how are we going to convince him this is a good idea? What—?"

"I'll give it a try."

Once again, Izumi broke in with great determination.

"Oh, okay. I'll leave it to you, then!"

Hinami must have learned her lesson, because this time, she handed Izumi the baton without a fight. Izumi had finally gained the inner strength to bend Hinami to her will. The power of love was even stronger than the perfect heroine.

I felt like this was a good job for her. After all, it was almost an established fact that they both liked each other.

"But wait, isn't it gonna be hard to get Shuji to see you?" Takei pointed out. Izumi giggled confidently.

"We have plans to go out this weekend! Shuji can be difficult sometimes, but he wouldn't stand me up at the last minute!"

Oh right, they had a date for the second week of September. But Izumi's belief in him wasn't quite ironclad just yet.

"…I don't think so, at least."

"Now you're not sure?" I asked, making an effort to tease her and get a laugh from the others. I was really just copying Nakamura's and Mizusawa's skill here. Mizusawa chuckled.

"Nah, I don't think he'd blow you off," he said, before adding a teasing "...Probably."

"Hey! Have a little more faith in us, Hiro!"

Everyone laughed at Izumi's reaction. Yeah, watching us speak back-to-back like this, it's obvious that Mizusawa still has the upper hand when it comes to messing with people. Gotta work on that.

Hinami looked at Izumi, her hand on her chin.

"You know the quiz is on Thursday, right? You don't mind studying before you check with Shuji?"

Her point was that if Nakamura didn't give us his approval, then it wouldn't matter if Izumi scored 90 percent or not. In other words, this could be a big waste of her time.

But for Izumi, Hinami's argument was trivial. She had already made up her mind.

"I know I may not need to, but if there's a chance it'll help, I want to do it."

"...Okay."

Izumi wanted to help Nakamura more than anything else, even if there was a chance her effort would be wasted. *See, Hinami? This is what it looks like to follow your heart.*

With our plan basically decided, Hinami started to wrap up the discussion.

"Well, the rest is up to Shuji now. If Yuzu can convince him, we'll use the plan we discussed to get his mom on board with *Atafami*. Case closed. If not...we'll come up with something else!"

"Agreed!"

Izumi was beaming. And with that, the strategy meeting came to an end.

* * *

That night, I was sitting at my desk in my room, studying math and reflecting on the events of the day. Hinami's overly rational approach to the problem had surprised me. But what stuck with me even more was the way Izumi was so intent on following her heart. The reason Izumi took action—her desire to help—was uniquely her own, but this wasn't the first time I'd seen something similar. I didn't think she was the only one who'd acted like this...

That was when I connected the dots between what Kikuchi-san had said to me at the café and the reason Izumi took action in the current situation.

"So that means..."

I had a small aha moment.

It wasn't quite the same as Konno and her fear of others looking down on her, but if my theory was correct, this new weapon could play a major role in my quest to defeat her.

Maybe I should be thinking more along these lines—but it probably wouldn't be enough. I'd just discovered another way to strike at Konno's weaknesses, but it wasn't a powerful enough weapon for a one-hit KO.

So do I need a way to strengthen it...or...?

I thought about it late into the night.

* * *

After school the next day, instead of the usual meeting with Hinami, I was attending a different kind of gathering: a study session for Izumi and me, led by Hinami.

"Yep, yep. If you substitute there...see?"

"Oh, that makes sense."

Predictably, Hinami was a good teacher. She instantly intuited what I was having trouble with and knew exactly what to say to help me put it together. Instead of giving me the correct answer, she'd tell me just enough for me to realize my mistake, fix it, and have the satisfaction of solving the problem, which helped me remember the formulas much better, too. She made an excellent tutor. Plus, she was pretty.

But just as I was thinking that such a perfect teaching style would guarantee better grades for anyone, the exception to the rule popped up.

"Um...substitute for this 'X'?"

Izumi's brain was working so hard, I could almost see the steam coming from her ears.

"Right. And then you can use this formula, which we just went over..."

"Um...which one was that again?"

"It's... Okay, here—"

"Oh...I-I'm sorry."

Izumi was having more trouble than I'd expected. She was getting more and more dejected until finally, she was reduced to apologies, and the tension was starting to rise. But Hinami just turned to her with a slightly teasing, mischievous smile.

"Yuzu...how in the world did you get into our high school?"

"Sh-shut up!"

The two of them burst into giggles. The mood lightened.

Wow. That was a completely insignificant exchange, but it was incredible to me. Instead of following Izumi's lead with something like *Don't worry about it!* Hinami had lightened the mood by teasing her for being a hopeless student. It was a very advanced skill.

The funny thing was, her approach ended up creating the impression that it didn't matter. If she'd said we still had time or she shouldn't worry, it would have added more weight to the failure by suggesting she didn't want to hurt Izumi's feelings. Her tactic produced a better result, but it was a bit too advanced for me to copy at this stage. I think she was able to pull it off because she perfectly controlled her tone and expression. If I tried the same thing, it would probably come across as a low blow and hurt Izumi even more.

Izumi laced her fingers together and stretched her hands high over her head.

"I just happened to do well on the Hokushin test and got in on early admission. This was actually the only place I applied to."

"Oh, really?"

I listened from the sidelines, thinking about Saitama's mysterious early-admission system. A couple times a year, junior high kids took the Hokushin, a prefectural scholastic aptitude test. If you did well on that, you were virtually guaranteed to pass the high school entrance exam.

Basically, if your two best scores were above a certain level, you could count on passing the exam. Also, it was easier to pass if you only applied to one school. Izumi must have lucked out and made it to our school by scoring high enough on her top two tests and getting the bonus for only applying here. Welcome to the dark side of Saitama Prefecture.

"Yeah… But I think I'm starting to get this math stuff! Thanks, Aoi-sensei!"

Hinami made a pained expression. "I've gotta head to practice soon. Are you gonna be okay?"

"Oh right! I've gotta go, too!" Izumi said, hurriedly packing her bag.

"So for the rest, will everyone just study on their own?" Hinami asked us, sticking her notebook into her already packed bag and slinging it onto her shoulder. She was even efficient about this.

"Yeah, I think so…"

Izumi shut her notebook uncertainly and stuffed it into her bag. I couldn't help thinking she'd have a tough time studying enough tonight to get a ninety on the test the following day. Hinami probably thought Izumi didn't need to do that well as long as the two of us did, and that was why she wasn't pushing her too hard. Which was true, if you were only concerned about solving Nakamura's problem.

But the thing I wanted to avoid the most was for Izumi to fail in what she wanted, which in this case was to get a high score. It might be a silly goal, but I could feel something indefinable in my heart saying I needed to go for it.

That's why I did what I did next.

"Um, Hinami?"

"…Huh? What?"

Hinami turned to me and answered just a moment too late. She might have known she wouldn't like where this was going—and if she did, she was right. I scrunched my face into a look of concern instead of a grin and told her my idea.

"I'm still feeling a little shaky on some points, so I was wondering if we could go to a diner or something to study some more after your practice."

"Uh… I won't get out till late…," she said, not giving a clear yes or no.

"I was just gonna study in the library and go meet you whenever you're done."

"Oh, really?" she said with clear displeasure. Now came the meat of my proposal. I looked at Izumi.

"If you've still got questions, too, you wanna come with us?"

Her eyes lit up. "If it's okay with you, Aoi, that would be a real lifesaver!"

Anyone could have guessed her feelings from the sparkles in her eyes—she was counting on Hinami from the bottom of her heart. It was next to impossible for Hinami to see all that hope and turn her down. She'd proven that much several times the day before.

"...Okay then, let's all meet up afterward!"

She accepted our plan with a well-guarded smile, and I could almost hear her yelling *Goddammit, Tomozaki!* at me in her head. But I'd done it. Now Izumi would have a fighting chance at getting a top score.

After Izumi used the power of hope to defeat Hinami, I hunkered down in the library to study for a while. When Hinami was available again, we met at a diner near school, got another great tutoring session from her, and headed home.

Well, I'd done everything I could. Now we just had to take the quiz.

Man, following my heart was fun. The world seemed a little brighter and more colorful—and I don't think I was imagining things.

* * *

It was break time before math class on the day of the test. Izumi was on edge. Her eyes were puffy, and she was gulping down a can of black coffee to drown her sleepiness. She grimaced with every sip. She probably hated coffee and only bought it because that's what people do when they're tired.

"...I hope this goes okay..." Shivering like a puppy, she went over the notes from the day before again and again.

"You'll be fine! Think about how much you studied!" Hinami said encouragingly.

"Y-yeah," I added. "Honestly, I'm worried, too..."

"Tomozaki-kun. We're focusing on Izumi right now, okay?"

"Huh? Oh yeah, r-right… You'll be fine, Izumi."

"Uhhh, that wasn't very convincing!"

"Yuzu, why don't you go over the problems I showed you yesterday? The ones that are most likely to be on the test."

"Ooh, good idea!"

"Y-yeah!"

"I wasn't talking to you, Tomozaki-kun…"

Under Hinami's watchful eye, the two of us looked over our notes until the end of break. As soon as class started, the math teacher handed out the quizzes, and I got to work on the rows of numbers. I was slightly more nervous than usual, but I muddled through all the questions.

Compared with our other quizzes so far, this one seemed slightly harder. But thanks to Hinami's tutoring, I was fairly confident in all my answers. And she was right about a bunch of the problems she said would probably be on the test. I'm bad at math, but this time, I think I might have aced it.

When the time was up, we handed in our tests, and the teacher quickly looked through them. In the meantime, I leaned over to Izumi.

"…How'd it go?" I whispered.

Her lips pressed together tightly, she nodded a few times.

"Well, I'm not a hundred percent sure I couldn't do it. So I can definitely say I don't know," she said in a rather clipped tone. Huh?

"Uh…so I guess we just have to wait for the results."

"Yep. That's all we can do."

"…Yeah."

Maybe because she'd used part of her brain that she didn't usually use, or maybe because she was anxious about the results, Izumi was acting stiffer than usual. I decided to leave her alone and focus on class.

Izumi, I really hope you reach your goal, even if it's by a hair…

* * *

The next day was super embarrassing.

"Congratulations, Yuzu! You make your tutor proud!"

"Thanks! I really have you to thank!"

Izumi threw her arms around Hinami, who patted her head. This time, Izumi let her do it without insisting she wasn't a baby.

During the break after our math quizzes were handed back, the three of us had gathered with Mizusawa and Takei to go over our scores. Of course, Izumi and I had already shown each other what we got, since we sit right next to each other. Anyway, the all-important scores…

Hinami: 100 percent.

Izumi: 95 percent.

Me: 85 percent.

Meaning this little strategy ended with everyone but me achieving their goal. What was I thinking the previous day? *I* was the one who didn't reach my goal, and by quite a bit more than a hair.

"Aw, don't sweat it, Farm Boy!"

"Fumiya… Well, it wasn't a horrible score…"

"Sh-shut up! I told you, math isn't my thing!" I snapped back, playing up the despair. All four of them laughed. Well, that went over well. The area of effect for my skills must be improving with practice. Now if I could just expand it to the whole class, that would be huge.

Hinami seemed pleased by the results.

"But anyway, two of us scored over ninety, and Tomozaki-kun… Well, he didn't quite hit the target, but his score was still good. I think we'll be able to make a convincing case!"

I was sure her smile had much less to do with the support for our argument and more to do with her sadistic pleasure in my low score. Still, I turned to Izumi and nodded.

"So now all you have to do is tell Nakamura about the plan."

"Right!"

Izumi nodded back, her smile full of that freedom and relief that came with completing a difficult task. It *was* impressive to think she'd gone from being that bad at math to acing her test—all thanks to how strong her desire to help Nakamura was. This was her special gift. Of course, what right does the worst scorer have to be thinking about it at all?

Hinami slapped Izumi's back lightly.

"Good luck talking Shuji into our plan this weekend!" she said.

"Of course! I got this!"

Izumi patted her own chest with new confidence. I felt like she'd just taken a step up toward the next tier. I also felt like her chest jiggled a little when she patted it. Wait, what am I talking about?!

* * *

The following Monday, I had a quick morning meeting with Hinami, then I headed to our classroom. The members of the Nakamura Crisis Team, including Hinami, were already together by the back windows. Most likely, Izumi was giving them the rundown on her date with Nakamura over the weekend.

"Man, you're late, Farm Boy!"

"Oh, uh, sorry."

Actually, I'd gotten to Sewing Room #2 early, and the only reason I was late now was because Hinami had headed to class first…so Takei's comment struck me as slightly absurd, but my only option was to apologize.

"I told Shuji everything, just like I promised! I told him I studied my butt off even though I hate math and got a ninety-five, and he got all grumpy and called me stupid! You can't get a ninety-five if you're stupid, though, right?"

"I don't think that's what he meant," I shot back. Izumi brightened right up.

"Anyway, he said to 'do whatever,' so we're okay to move forward with the plan! I was just telling everyone I think we should go to his house today!"

"Oh yeah?"

"Yeah!"

So Nakamura's "*do whatever*" meant *yes*? Normie language was hard. Putting that aside, I was happy about Izumi's good news. As I watched Izumi bask in her success, I remembered the other thing I'd been wondering about.

"But…how did the date go?" I asked her.

"C'mon, it wasn't a *date*!"

Her face turned bright red. Talking about romance was a weak point for her. Her and everyone alive, really.

"I was wondering about that, too! Give us the deets, Yuzucchi!" Takei said.

"Um, well…"

As Izumi was trying to avoid answering, a massive pair of hands reached out and grabbed her head, messing up her pretty, dyed-brown hair.

"'Sup?"

The owner of the hands was Nakamura. *Wait, Nakamura?!* I did a double take. We were all staring at him as he let her go. For some reason, Takei's eyes were filled with tears.

"…Shuji!!"

Takei grabbed Nakamura by the shoulders and shook him back and forth. Nakamura didn't look happy about it, but he didn't brush him off immediately.

"…Stop it already, man!" he finally said, elbowing Takei when he'd had enough.

"Owww!" Takei yelped, a huge smile on his face.

So Nakamura was back. Which meant the problem was solved before Hinami ever implemented her plan.

"Hey. What's it been, a week?"

Mizusawa looked at Nakamura with a smile of defeat.

"I just skipped a couple days; you guys are making way too big a deal out of this. I don't get why you studied super hard just to argue with my mom."

Nakamura scratched his head roughly.

"What are you talking about? We busted our butts for you!"

Hinami elbowed him teasingly. She was one of the few people who could tease him naturally. I'd done it a couple of times as an assignment, but I could never pull it off the way she could.

"Yeah, yeah, fine. Thanks. Aren't you already good at math?"

"Yeah, but I had to work hard to teach these two!"

"Fine, I'll give you that. Not like I asked you to."

Nakamura made sure his thanks came along with some snark. What he was saying was logical enough, and he probably didn't want to come across as *too* humble. Some good lessons there.

Izumi was standing next to Nakamura, shooting him shy glances.

"...Morning."

Finally, she sighed out a quiet, vulnerable greeting for his ears alone, blushing and peering up at him through her lashes.

"...Hey."

She seemed to have had an effect, because Nakamura looked away and sounded the tiniest bit embarrassed when he answered. *How can you two turn a simple* good morning *into flirting? That's communication on a whole different level.* Even as dense as he was, Nakamura must have realized how much effort Izumi put in over the past couple days. Of course he would feel embarrassed. He quickly rallied, however.

"But come on, you worry too much. What the hell, getting a ninety-five on the quiz?"

And now he was needling Izumi, too. I think it might actually kill him to be honest for once.

"What?! You made us so worried, and that's all you can say?!"

"You always get a ton of problems wrong! It's just a weird way of helping," he said bluntly. Maybe I was imagining it, but I thought I saw a very un-Nakamura-like glint of kindness deep in his eyes.

"That's so mean! It was all *your* fault!"

"Yeah, yeah. Anyway, I'm not skipping school anymore, so you can cut it out with all this," he said lightly, flicking Izumi's forehead.

"Ouch! Stop it!" Izumi protested, but Nakamura had already turned to Mizusawa and started a different conversation. She stared at his back with a mixture of anger and reassurance.

I realized something as I watched her. The reason Nakamura was back in school had less to do with Hinami's rational strategy and more to do with Izumi's efforts. Her simple desire to help Nakamura got through to him. That's all there was to it. And that knowledge made me extremely happy.

The bell rang a few minutes later. We all wanted to keep talking, but we had to sit down. In the minutes before the teacher got to class, while everyone was chatting noisily, I heard someone whisper my name.

"Hey, Tomozaki!"

"...Yeah?"

I turned toward the voice. Izumi was looking down, somehow staring off into space with fire burning in her eyes.

"Uh, what's wrong?"

This was different than usual. She tightened her fingers around her pen on her desk, as if that fire was burning brighter minute by minute.

"I just had a thought."

As if whatever was possessing her had released her, she looked suddenly calm, with a quieter kind of excitement.

"What kind of thought...?"

She slowly turned toward me and looked me straight in the eye. "Well..." Her gaze was powerful. I'd noticed her new core of strength recently, but right now, that core suddenly seemed way stronger. I remembered what Kikuchi-san had said to me at the café in Omiya: *"You're facing the future more straightforwardly than you were before."* That's exactly how Izumi struck me at that moment.

"So...remember how I wasn't sure if I should help Hirabayashi-san or not?"

"Huh...? Oh right."

I nodded.

"I was on the fence at first, but not helping would be the same as letting Erika tell me what to do. I'd be letting the mood carry me along. I'd be the kind of person I'm trying not to be anymore."

She strung the words together little by little, awkwardly but steadily giving her feelings a concrete shape.

"Yeah...you did say that."

I sensed she'd arrived at an answer. My job right now was just to listen. I had to become the bottom-tier character again and hear her out without getting in the way.

"But…I realized right now I was wrong."

"Wrong about what?"

Izumi reached over to her right hand and squeezed her fingers.

"I did everything I did because I wanted to help Shuji, right?"

"Yes…"

She seemed to be working out her feelings as she spoke.

"I did everything I wanted, like volunteering to talk to his mom and studying math. I got Aoi and everyone to help me, and…I went a little crazy. Like, geez, chill out, right?"

She covered up her embarrassment with a little joke.

"Maybe—you were really going for it."

I couldn't help smiling as I thought back to how she'd been acting lately. True enough, she was so intense about this that Hinami was powerless against her. To say nothing of the studying for math.

"Ah-ha-ha. Thought so. I was on overdrive, and now I'm kinda regretting it…"

"Ha-ha-ha…really?"

In a sense, she'd lost sight of reason.

"But at the same time…Shuji came back to school after all that. And I realized something."

"Mm-hmm?"

She looked down at her chest like she was trying to see into her heart.

"It seems obvious, but…I did everything because I just wanted to help Shuji, right?"

"…Yeah."

"No one told me to do it, right?"

"Nope, no one did."

Izumi took a deep breath. "So I think the same should go for Hirabayashi-san."

"…How so?"

She looked back at me.

*   *   *

“Erika tried to make me captain, but that doesn’t matter. I want to help Hirabayashi-san, so I’m going to help her. That’s it!”

I was fairly surprised to hear that.

“Really…? So you’ll just do what you want?”

She nodded deeply again.

“Yeah. I don’t care about the mood. If I want to help her, then I should help her. That’s what I want to do!”

Her words and expression were gentle, yet firm and powerful, like a willow tree. She looked at Hirabayashi-san, who sat near the front of the classroom.

“I’m going to ask her if she wants me to take over the role of captain. If she still says she’ll do it, then I’ll leave it to her, but I think she’s probably having a really rough time with Erika.”

Her voice was full of resolve, as if the fog had cleared.

“…Huh, that could be a good approach.”

“I think so… Thanks for listening to me, Tomozaki! I feel better now!”

Her tone clearly required major skill—soft, but full of energy—and her charming smile was like a ray of sunlight.

“Er, I mean…you’re welcome.”

“Oh, also,” she said, lowering her voice. “Let’s keep working on Erika, too.”

She smiled mischievously and jokingly raised one finger. Her expression was as cheerful as a sunflower, but filled with a light that was uniquely Izumi’s.

The teacher had arrived, and class was about to start, but I nodded back at Izumi.

“Sure thing!”

She grinned and then turned toward the front of the class.

Interesting.

I mulled it over for a bit.

Even when everyone had been trying to pin the role of captain on someone else—

Even though the class queen had tried to force her into doing it—
Even though she'd rather not do it—
Even though doing it would require sacrificing herself—
Even then.

If she wanted to help someone and made the choice herself, then she wasn't succumbing to the mood or someone else's will.

It was an act she chose herself, thanks to her own steadfast will.

That was a discovery she had made on her own. From an outside perspective, it probably didn't look like a dramatic change. You could even say her actions themselves took her back to her old self—helping someone in trouble and taking on a job no one else wanted.

But it was what she wanted to do. And that was why she was able to walk down her own path so confidently.

When I realized that, I was filled with admiration for Yuzu Izumi's strength. She had found how she wanted to live and grabbed hold of it.

"Damn…she's one strong character," I murmured, nodding at my own conclusion.

4

Even seemingly unbeatable bosses have weak points

During the first-period break on the day Nakamura came back, Hinami, Izumi, and I joined his group by the back window to finish our conversation from earlier. We were chatting noisily when a loud shout exploded from the front of the classroom.

"So you finally decided to come back, huh, Shuji? Don't you think a week is a little too much to skip?"

It was Erika Konno. She was sitting cross-legged on top of her desk, cackling like a classic trendsetter.

"Guess I felt like coming today," Nakamura shot back, and there was some weight behind it.

Erika Konno climbed down from her desk and walked straight up to him with two members of her posse.

"Seriously, though, why were you out for so long? Just tired of school?"

Konno's friends blended into our group by the back window, meaning the new group was made up of Hinami, Nakamura, Mizusawa, Takei, Izumi, Erika Konno, her two hangers-on, and me. Nine of us, and I was the only bottom-tier character. All of a sudden, I felt totally out of place, and I was getting the sense that I shouldn't say anything.

"Yeah, kinda. As long as I make it to third year, I'm good, right?" Nakamura said intimidatingly. It was like the showdown in the old principal's office. Konno and Nakamura were terrifying when they talked to each other…

This was max difficulty here. As far as what I could do here—well, observation was about it. I wanted to join in on the conversation, but that was obviously impossible. I mean, I went off on the queen before, and I

hadn't talked to her since. *Shit. Wish I could just slip away from this little meeting.*

"Why's Tomozaki here? Kinda out of place."

Just as all those thoughts were running through my head, Konno put me right in my bottom-tier place. *Ugh, stop it. I know I don't fit in. I want to disappear; you don't have to rub salt in the wound.* Her words got to me because I more or less agreed. Or… *Erika Konno-san, you aren't still mad about that fight, are you? Figures. I gave you hell.*

"Sh-shut up. I'm not out of place. I'm right here."

I guess my gamer's hatred of losing took control and made me want to fight back a little, and I *had* been practicing messing with people. And that's how I ended up saying something really dumb. I think that was the world's dumbest response to being told I was out of place.

"…Huh?"

When she turned her frown on me, all my fighting spirit evaporated. I was like a deer in the headlights. Like a random NPC when the dragon attacks. No chance of survival. *Welp, I'm screwed.*

Mizusawa smiled and pointed at Konno's hair.

"Hey, Erika, did you curl your hair yourself?"

"Oh, can you tell? You're sharp, Takahiro." She petted her hair.

"What can I say? You're almost as good as me."

"What?! Shut up!"

The conversation rolled on smoothly. *Nice one, Mizusawa.* He'd pushed her buttons on her favorite topic—beauty—added just the right dash of teasing, and expertly seized control of the conversation. As I was replaying the series of events in my head, I realized something. That analysis was a sign of some fairly significant improvement. I'd been working on observation day in and day out lately, which was probably why I was noticing this little stuff.

"What, too cheap to pay for a perm?" Nakamura said.

"Huh? I'd rather spend the money on clothes. Right, Yuzu?"

"Yeah, we went shopping together the other day! I keep buying so much stuff, it's crazy…"

"I get you! I'm like that with food…," Hinami said.

"You mean cheese, right?" Mizusawa teased.

"Ah-ha-ha, nooo, don't share my secrets!"

"Seriously! You eat so much cheese whenever we go anywhere!" Takei jumped in.

The conversation hurtled on. I couldn't join in, so I focused all my energy on observing. As I watched the eight of them talk, I picked up on a couple of points. It was mostly vague stuff like who was looking where, the combination of what they were saying and their body language, and various inferences based on information I'd already collected. But still…

If what I noticed was right, I had the feeling that I'd finally found the last key to clearing Hinami's assignment.

* * *

During the break before we went to class in another room, I went to the library for the first time in ages. Lately, I'd been busy with my assignment, and I had the option of seeing Kikuchi-san on the weekends, so I hadn't been here in a while. Today, though, I wanted to talk to her about something.

I slowly pushed open the door and looked inside. She was sitting at her usual table in her usual chair, quietly reading a book. When she was surrounded by books, she had a uniquely intellectual, holy presence that was also a warm and pure presence. Like there was a sacred flame burning in her—that was probably the easiest way to put it. Kikuchi-san wasn't in the library; the library had arisen with her at its center. At least, that's how it felt to me.

As I stepped into her world, our eyes met. I walked slowly and calmly up to her, sat down next to her, paused to take a breath, and then looked her in the eye again. Her kind smile, peaceful as the night sky in autumn, struck something deep in my soul.

"…Hi."

She greeted me with a voice like the soft tapping of fingernails on a church bell—delicate and profound but also elegant and welcoming.

"…Hi."

My voice began with a quiet breath delicately vibrating my vocal cords, amplified in the resonant chambers of my throat and nose.

By the way, the reason I'm describing my voice in terms of the body's physical structure is because coming here alone feels like coming home to Kikuchi-san—it feels like I can finally relax.

"It's good that Nakamura-kun is back," Kikuchi-san said with a gentle smile. I nodded, thinking about how observant she was with our class.

"Yeah," I said.

Kikuchi-san smiled mischievously. "And you had a hand in that, didn't you?"

Her tone was teasing but warm. Recently, she'd been doing that a lot. The impression wasn't devilish or angelic—just very human. Very Kikuchi-san. It made me happy because I could tell she was opening her heart to me.

"Yeah, you could say that..."

"Hee-hee...I thought so," she said, smiling brightly and nodding slowly in an almost loving way, like she was affirming my whole self. "Good job."

Wrapped in her motherly aura, like getting a pat on the head, I could feel the bashfulness coming on, and I started talking in order to hide it.

"B-but...it was really Izumi who did all the work."

"Izumi-san..."

She rested her chin softly on the top edge of her book and looked up, thinking quietly.

"...What's the matter?" I asked, still a ball of nerves. She blushed and glanced around. A few people were sitting nearby. She pressed her book to her lips and brought her face to my ear, like she was about to tell me a secret.

"Izumi-san and Nakamura-kun like each other, don't they?"

Thanks to her breathy, incredibly delicate whisper, my right and left brains instantly melted together so that all I could do was nod mechanically.

"Yeah."

My overheated neurons barely managed to produce a single, monotone syllable before creaking to a halt. My MP (mental points) was dropping to zero, or maybe I should say the healing power had been too much for me and just wiped it out… I dunno, man. I have no idea what I'm talking about.

Kikuchi-san hugged her book to her chest and giggled.

"I hope it goes well for them. I'm a bit envious."

Her good-willed smile was pure and honest, and her own yearning for love was completely noble. *Thank you, Kikuchi-san's parents—thank you, planet Earth, for giving birth to this girl.* These were the thoughts passing through my mind with utter seriousness as I watched her smile. More accurately speaking, these were the thoughts I was trying to focus on to cool down my overheated face.

Funnily enough, Nakamura was one of the topics I'd wanted to ask her about today. I refocused my attention on the business at hand.

"Um…can I get your opinion about something?"

* * *

After school that day, I headed to Sewing Room #2. It was the first time Hinami and I had met alone since Nakamura came back to school.

"Now that the Nakamura situation has been sorted out, I'd like to quickly review that and then focus on the Konno assignment." Hinami sighed, stroking the hair resting on her shoulders. I bet the stress from all that illogical planning was building up in her.

"Gotcha. Well, the route may not have been the most rational, but the outcome was fantastic," I answered, needling her with just a bit of irony. Hinami smiled like she relished the challenge.

"Listen to you! Well, you certainly did a wonderful job of leading everyone into wasting their time and effort," she calmly retorted.

"Thanks," I replied, just as sarcastic. "I did have a few thoughts about that, though."

I wanted to talk about all this heart-following stuff, which was my top priority. Hinami's eyes turned serious.

"Was all that pointless meandering what you consider staying true to what you want?" she asked provocatively, staring into the depths of my eyes.

I realized this was an important moment.

That time Hinami and I argued, I'd talked about *what I really wanted.* I was certain she was using this situation as another opportunity to decide whether that was something that was even measurable. It's a common argument to say that being logical all the time is just suffocating and cold, but that's emotion-based. If I said that, Hinami wouldn't even want to consider my side of the argument.

I carefully organized my thoughts before answering her.

"Well, this is just a theory, or like...one of several possible arguments."

"...Uh-huh."

My proof-oriented tone must have gotten me over the first hurdle, because Hinami shifted her posture into listening mode and nodded. It would be impossible to prove my point unless I did it in her ring—with logic.

"Anyway, here's my thoughts about what happened. You were making rapid-fire suggestions on how to solve the Nakamura problem using the most rational and quickest approach, right?"

"Yes, I was."

"But Izumi and I kept interrupting you with our silly ideas, so you weren't able to fully do it your way."

"Precisely. I don't even know how many times I gave in..."

Hinami sighed. As I suspected, the experience had exhausted her. My hope was that it was the first step toward pulling off her steadfast mask.

"Yes, you did give in a lot. But..."

"But what?"

Again, she gave me a look like she was challenging me, and I tried to break through my words.

"If you hadn't given in—if you'd pushed ahead with your own approach...I think the problem would have taken even longer to solve. Don't you agree?"

Hinami blinked a few times.

"...What are you talking about? That's obvious. I mean, I wanted to wait until Nakamura came to us for help."

I shook my head.

"That's not what I mean. I mean after that."

"...After?"

In other words, after we'd decided to start laying the groundwork to help Nakamura before getting his go-ahead. Even when we were taking a less straightforward path, Hinami had tried to apply her logic.

"Don't you think if we'd done everything you said after that, solving the problem would have taken longer? I mean, you were trying to get us to convince Nakamura's mom that playing *Atafami* wasn't bad—in order to solve the problem of the *Atafami* ban, right?"

"What do you mean? Wasn't that the problem that needed solving?" she said, as if it was obvious. But I just pointed back at her.

"Well, we never did solve the problem of the *Atafami* ban, did we?"

Hinami nodded twice, slowly, and smiled like she was enjoying this argument.

"Aha, I see what you're saying."

I nodded back at her.

"Yeah, I think you're with me now. The *Atafami* ban was the source of the fight, but like I said, it was never resolved. But we were still able to get Nakamura back in school within less than a week of launching our plan. This was the shortest possible route to a solution—and one that your logic didn't find."

"Ah, I see." Hinami raised her eyebrows happily.

"I think you already know this, but the key was Izumi's desire to help Nakamura. And because he realized how she felt, he came back to school even though the root problem wasn't fixed. If we'd followed your method, we'd have had to wait until that root problem was resolved to get him to come back. Your way would have taken longer."

"I'll admit, that's fair."

She was resting her chin in her hand, but her eyes blazed with fighting spirit. I met them head-on.

"You set these goals based on your own rules, but you're unable to step outside of the rational approach. But when you follow your instincts and do what you want to do, you can find shortcuts that you wouldn't otherwise. That's what happened this time."

Hinami nodded again.

"I see. So what you want to say is, your and Yuzu's desires were effective in finding the shortest route."

"Right."

I nodded. She thought for a moment, finger on her lips, then smiled sadistically.

"I give you a score of sixty percent."

I yelped with indignation. "Wh-what?"

She looked at me with complete and utter calm.

"Think about it. You're trying to argue for following your heart over logic, right?"

"Huh? Well, yeah, right now I am."

Hinami shook her head. "It's weird. You're saying you should follow your heart because it allows you to find the shortest possible route to your goal."

"...So?"

Hinami sighed, as if to say *You don't get it?*

"You're saying it's great because it allows you to find the shortest possible route. But you're ultimately just saying it's great because it's rational, right?"

"...Oh."

Her point dawned on me.

"You wanted to explain why focusing on what you want, on something irrational, is so great, right? But you ended up essentially saying you found a method that's more rational than mine. Which makes you even more of a logical extremist than me."

She was right. I'd wanted to say that by pursuing what you want, you could achieve something more wonderful than was possible through logic alone. In which case, I should have shown how it could give you

something Hinami's approach couldn't. But without even noticing it, I'd ended up arguing that my way was just more rational, which was to say, I'd fallen into a value system that said logic was better.

"Y-yeah, that's true...," I groaned. Hinami looked at me, apparently pleased to see me speechless. Her smile was devilish and extremely amused.

"Well, you get the picture. It wasn't a bad attempt. Better luck next time. If you're going to argue for the merits of prioritizing what you want, you need to show me something I can't get by doing it my way," she chided, poking my cheek like she was my big sister. *Ugh, shit. This is just embarrassing.*

"B-but it's hard to find the most effective method just doing it your way, isn't it? Aren't there some approaches you can only discover using my way? I mean, we wouldn't have achieved the results we did this time otherwise..." I was refusing to admit I'd lost.

"Okay. If that's the case, then prioritizing rationality isn't bad in itself—we just set the wrong goals this time around. Sure, things turned out this way because I made getting rid of the *Atafami* ban my goal, but what if I'd focused on getting Nakamura to stop skipping school instead? We would have been able to take a variety of approaches, including communicating Yuzu's feelings to Nakamura, right?"

Hinami smiled triumphantly.

"At least, *I* would have been able to," she added.

"Damn..."

That was all I could say. She was right that simply by shifting the goal, she would have had a whole bunch of options: having Izumi call Nakamura to say she was worried about him, using the ever-straightforward Takei, or... Well, that was about all I could come up with, but anyway, she could have made a plan and achieved results just as fast as we had this time.

As long as she didn't mess up setting the goal, she could reach the same territory through her extremely rational approach that we could reach only by chance through ours.

That was her version of "correctness."

* * *

Some people made the mistake of setting goals in pursuit of mechanical, numerical efficiency only, so their version of logic ended up ignoring emotions entirely. And that made it weaker.

But the final boss, Aoi Hinami, mechanically and numerically included emotions in the calculations that formed the basis for her pursuit of efficiency, which she in turn incorporated into her overall rational approach.

In which case, she had no need for my approach. At least, not for the reason I'd just given.

Hinami tapped her chin twice with her pointer finger, looking happy.

"That's why I gave you sixty percent. I'll admit, your argument was quite a bit better than some others you could have come up with. Some people might slap together an argument by insisting something's self-evident when it isn't—like a religion or something. You made a genuine effort to prove your point. That was fun."

Hinami's little speech was getting kinda high-handed, but she had me beat.

"...B-but why'd you mess up the goal this time? I think you failed to see that Nakamura coming back to school was the most important thing. And you missed it because your thinking was overly rational, no?"

Hinami looked more pleased than ever as she responded.

"Oh, no... It was the opposite, actually."

"...Wh-what do you mean?"

She looked at me triumphantly.

"I wanted to stop Nakamura's mother from thinking *Atafami* rots your brain."

She smiled sadistically.

"Oh..."

By pointing out exactly how her irrational feelings toward *Atafami* had led her to a more time-consuming solution, Hinami declared a decisive victory. She was just too strong.

* * *

That night, I was eating dinner with my family and thinking over my assignment. I was fairly sure I'd discovered Erika Konno's weakness by watching Izumi work to help Nakamura, but I didn't think I could deliver a one-hit KO with that alone.

I would need another trick to help conquer her.

There was her desire for people to not look down on her, and then there was the strange feeling I'd noticed when Nakamura came back to school.

I connected all the dots and put the finishing touches on my plan, for what it was. What I ended up with was such a classic bottom-tier-character strategy that I was half-afraid Hinami would get mad at me for even suggesting it. But I figured this was the only way to take down a boss like Erika Konno.

My strategy was extremely simple.

If I couldn't take her down with a single arrow, then I'd keep shooting until she finally fell.

I sat on my bed, organizing my thoughts and going over what I needed to do. Before I knew it, I was asleep.

The next day, at my morning meeting with Hinami, I went over the points I needed to confirm before implementing my plan.

"I'd like to review a few things about my assignment with you."

"Like what?"

I mentally reviewed my strategy.

"At our meeting the other day, you said asking other people for help was a good approach to this assignment, right?"

Hinami nodded. "Right. Since Erika Konno is such a powerful opponent, there are things you'll have a hard time handling with your skills alone."

"Exactly," I said, nodding. "…So about that…"

Hinami nodded encouragingly. I paused, then continued.

"Can I ask you to help?"

She looked at me suspiciously. "What exactly do you mean by 'help'?" she asked.

"Don't worry, I'm not going to ask you to tell me what to do… I just want to ask you to do something, and have you do it for me."

In other words, I'd be the one gripping the controller, and Hinami would be one of the characters I was using. I'd still be the gamer, here.

"…Ah, I see," Hinami said, apparently satisfied, and paused for a minute. "In that case, I'm okay with it."

"Oh, really?"

She nodded.

"Yeah. Just know I'm not going to say anything, even if I think your plan will fail. I'll do what you ask me to, and no more."

I nodded.

"Yes, that's all I want."

"Otherwise—"

I interrupted, pointing at her. "The assignment is meaningless?"

"…Well, yes."

She seemed extremely irritated by my cockiness, but I decided not to worry about it. I knew to expect as much.

"Oh, but you care what people think of you, so make sure that's not a problem."

"Obviously. I won't do anything embarrassing."

"Good. Anyway, about my strategy…" I filled her in.

"Got it. I can handle that. I'll start today."

"Okay. I appreciate it!"

Now that I had Hinami's approval, the meeting came to a close. Right! Time to lay the groundwork.

I headed to our classroom and looked around. Izumi had just arrived and was heaving her books onto her desk. Now was my chance to talk to her. This was the second phase of preparation. Plus, what was the situation with Hirabayashi-san? I wanted to ask her about that, too.

"Izumi."

"Oh, hey, Tomozaki!" she responded at several times my volume.

"Oh, uh, hey!" I said, flustered, as she switched into a dramatic, formal tone.

"I am now the captain!"

"...Oh, wow!"

It sounded like she'd talked to Hirabayashi-san and taken over her role. A woman of her word. Now that she'd found her way, she was a powerhouse.

"So it's all you, huh?" I said.

"Yeah, she was really struggling. And on the actual day of the tournament, the captain has to do stuff like trade out players and call time-outs. She said she was super nervous about that."

"...Huh. So it was good that you took over, then."

"Yeah!" she said with a strange sense of excitement. She was really wound up. "Oh, so what did you want to talk about?"

"Oh right. Actually..."

I lowered my voice.

"What?"

"It's about Erika Konno..."

I told her about my strategy, and she frowned.

"...You think that's all it'll take?"

Not a very good reaction—but I'd expected that.

"I can see why you're worried, but there's more to it than that..."

I explained my combo strategy, which was the core of my plan.

"Ah, now I get it! That makes more sense. That could work!"

"R-really?!" I was clinging to Izumi's encouragement.

"You should be more confident!"

"Y-yeah, I know."

I could feel Izumi's exasperation. But how was I supposed to feel confident when I was going up against someone as strong as Erika Konno?

Anyway, I'd gotten Hinami and Izumi to agree to help. Now I just had to tell Mizusawa about my plan.

"Well, I hope it works!" Izumi said.

I nodded. "Me too. Okay, I'm off to talk to Mizusawa."

"Oh, you haven't told him yet? I'll do it right now, then!" she said energetically.

"Huh?"

"Hiro!"

With almost impulsive speed, she called out to Mizusawa, who was talking with Nakamura's group.

"'Sup?"

Mizusawa being Mizusawa, he immediately slipped away from the conversation and walked over to us. Normies tend to be very decisive when it comes to communication.

"Tomozaki and I were just strategizing about the sports tournament..."

"About the tournament? Why? Girls and guys are separate, right?"

He looked back and forth between the two of us suspiciously. Their momentum was starting to overwhelm me, but I managed to pull my wits together and explain the situation to Mizusawa. "Uh, that's not quite what's going on. Actually..."

When I was done explaining, Mizusawa smirked.

"Sometimes I really do think you're secretly evil."

"Sh-shut up!"

He was kind of right, so I didn't protest that strongly. I'd picked up a little of Hinami's ruthless pragmatism. But this time, I was also trying to help everyone enjoy the tournament, which was what Izumi and I both genuinely wanted. Plus, I wasn't planning to do anything terrible, so in my mind, it was fine. As long as the goal itself was honest, I was good.

"Hmm, hmm. Okay. So you want me to work with Yuzu on all this?"

"Basically. I hate to ask, but do you mind?"

"Leave it to me! We'll be your mood-reading duo."

"Ha-ha-ha! Okay, thanks."

With that, I had all three of them on board. And my work here was done.

Yup, you've got that right. For this assignment, I'd thought up the strategy, but the implementation was totally up to other people. Or I should say, as a weaker character, I'd run around collecting the items needed to bring down the dragon and then asked a bunch of high-level characters to use them. I felt slightly guilty for doing so little, but I'd gotten Hinami's permission to rely on other people for help, and she'd said anything went as long as I was the one holding the controller. I'd also gotten her approval for the plan itself, so all in all, it seemed like I was meeting the assignment's requirements.

A sense of accomplishment washed over me as I sat back and recalled what Kikuchi-san had told me the day before in the library—and what had become the core of my strategy.

* * *

"Um…can I get your opinion about something?"

I'd asked her the question after Kikuchi-san whispered that she thought Nakamura and Izumi liked each other. We'd already talked about Erika Konno once before, at the café, but I had more I wanted to know.

"Yes…about what?"

She could tell I was serious; she stuck a bookmark in her book and laid it on the table before turning back toward me.

"Um, thanks," I said. "Actually, it's about Erika Konno again…"

I'd made three guesses, and now I was looking for a way to confirm them. It would have been one thing if I was carrying out the plan myself, but since I was relying on other people so heavily, I wanted to be sure before I asked them to help. That was why I'd decided to ask the observant Kikuchi-san about a couple of things. Guesses I made on my own were unreliable, but if someone else had the same thoughts, then the chance I was right would skyrocket.

"Hmm, what should I ask you first…? Okay, I'll start here."

"I'm listening."

I told her my first conjecture.

"The other day at the café, you said Erika Konno cares about her friends, right?"

"Yes…"

She nodded.

"Why do you think that is?"

When Kikuchi-san told me Erika Konno didn't want people to

look down on her, she'd followed up by saying she did care about her friends. At first, I assumed she was just saying that, but thinking more about it, I realized Kikuchi-san wasn't the type of person to say things she didn't mean. Then when I saw Izumi working so desperately to help Nakamura—when I witnessed her kindness up close—I remembered a certain characteristic that the most successful people share.

Take the time Mizusawa and Mimimi came to my house and started seriously discussing the romantic potential between Nakamura and Izumi. Or the time Hinami gave me her bag but acted like she was "trading" it for a little pin so I wouldn't feel guilty. Or the way Mimimi always acted like a goofball to protect Tama-chan. I'd learned from experience that normies, especially those at the top of the group, were often capable of genuine thoughtfulness.

Of course, there were exceptions, and maybe it was just a coincidence that the normies I knew were like that. But Erika Konno was the leader of a top-level group. From experience and from what Kikuchi-san had said, I might have found a possible route to success, no matter how scary she was.

"Well…," Kikuchi-san said with a slightly troubled smile. It didn't take long to figure out why. "For example, if someone's making fun of one of her good friends, she'll protect her friend by making fun of the other girl even more… And if one of her friends is rejected by a guy, she'll pick on him…"

"Oh…ha-ha."

I chuckled a little wryly. Kikuchi-san's examples were a demonstration of Konno's eye-for-an-eye approach, but I also realized she was right to say that was a form of thoughtfulness, too. Konno seemed to be attacking people for no reason, but she was actually doing it for the sake of her friends. It took speaking with Kikuchi-san for me to see that.

And that's when my first strategy took form.

I'd get Izumi to tell Erika Konno directly that she wanted everyone to have fun at the sports tournament.

* * *

That was my first weapon. Izumi was a close friend of hers, enough that they'd been shopping together multiple times already. As far as I could tell, Izumi was closer with Erika Konno than anyone else in her group. If Izumi told her straight up that she wanted to enjoy the tournament, it ought to have some impact—and all the more so if Konno cared about her friends.

Simply stating her feelings might sound like an easy job for Izumi, but keep in mind who she'd be telling this to. This was a fairly difficult mission. The strategy was only possible because she had grown so much lately and gotten better at speaking her mind. The weapon was only completed when Izumi became stronger. I'd better be grateful she leveled up.

"Thanks… And there's something else."

"Yes…" Kikuchi-san nodded, and I asked my next question.

"Erika Konno pays pretty close attention to Hinami, doesn't she? Y'know, as a rival?"

I waited for Kikuchi-san's response. She paused and looked down, like she wasn't sure what to say.

"Yes…I'd agree with that."

Okay. I had my second confirmation.

"Thought so."

I'd realized this on the day Erika Konno and her posse joined up with our group. I'd been observing the conversation between her, Nakamura, Mizusawa, Takei, Hinami, Izumi, and two of Konno's other hangers-on from outside the circle. Erika Konno and Hinami had hardly spoken to each other. I had never seen them talking before, but the way they even avoided making eye contact was just weird. And neither of them was quiet in the conversation overall, which must mean they were intentionally avoiding each other. And that meant there was an invisible but deep-rooted conflict between the leaders of the two groups.

If that conflict did exist, I couldn't imagine Hinami being the one to start it. The only scenario I could imagine was that Erika Konno initiated it, and Hinami went along because she didn't have any other options.

I didn't know if Konno viewed Hinami's brilliance in every area with hostility or plain old fear, but she definitely held some kind of negative emotion toward her. Ultimately, though, if I took Konno's pride into account, I'd bet she wanted to avoid taking an inferior position relative to someone stronger than her.

In other words, Konno saw Aoi Hinami as a greater rival than any of her other classmates. And that's where I'd aim my second weapon.

I'd make her think that if she didn't play well in the sports tournament, Hinami would look down on her.

I'd taken a hint from Hinami's own approach to problem-solving. For instance, with the Nakamura incident, she'd planned to use her own good grades to improve *Atafami*'s image. In the student council election, she'd used her achievements on the track team. All the effort she'd poured in beforehand produced major results. This time, I'd get her to use her high position in the class hierarchy.

All I had to do was ask Hinami flat-out to fan the flames of Erika Konno's insecurity, and the plan was as good as done. I'd asked her to make little comments to Konno's posse: *Is Erika going to play?* and *If she's not feeling up to it, she can leave it to me. I don't mind at all!* and *Guess this isn't really her thing, huh?* If the message reached Konno through them, that should spur her on somewhat. *Thank you, Hinami. I know the lines I'm giving you are kinda iffy.*

But this strategy wouldn't necessarily yield big results.

If Konno was able to avoid Hinami's contempt by making fun of the sports tournament, she could get what she wanted that way instead. To prevent this, I needed my third weapon.

And so I asked Kikuchi-san another question.

"Also…"

"Yes?"

I thought for a moment about how to phrase it.

"Erika Konno probably still likes Nakamura, don't you think?"

Kikuchi-san nodded a little reluctantly. "…I think so."

Okay. All the pieces were in place.

My reasons for that guess were simple. First, I'd heard her say in the old principal's office that she liked Nakamura in the past. Second, she'd showed her hand when he came back to school after his long absence.

The one and only Erika Konno had gotten up and walked over to join our group with no prompting whatsoever. It was strange for her. But when I thought about it, it all seemed very straightforward. She wanted to talk to Nakamura because he'd been away—and she wanted it so badly that instead of calling him over to her, she went to him.

This was my final weapon.

I'd get Mizusawa to smoothly drop a hint that Nakamura liked sporty girls.

It's kind of an idiotic plan, but some people say the simplest strategies work best. I don't really need to explain this one, right? The idea was to convince her that if she gave her all at the tournament, Nakamura might think she was hot. I had some qualms about using this weakness against her, but, well, sometimes the end justifies the means?

So that was my strategy, and I had a reason for using three prongs, thanks to what Gumi-chan had said at Karaoke Sevens. She belonged to the same tribe as Erika Konno, and she'd told me what was most important for conquering her.

"If you want to motivate the queen, you need to make it worth her while!"

In other words, cost performance was the key. Let me lay it out:

She wants to make her friend Izumi happy.
She wants to avoid having Aoi Hinami look down on her.
She wants Nakamura to like her.

Based on the information I'd collected, these were Erika Konno's three desires. I just had to set things up so that through the single action of getting involved in the sports tournament, she could fulfill all three of those desires. Once I did that, the payoff for that one little thing would be extra tempting.

Even if each individual element was weak, the three of them together packed quite a bit of punch, and the cost performance of participating improved. And when that happened, Erika Konno, Gumi-chan's fellow apathetic alien, would act.

That was my strategy to take down Erika Konno, made possible with the help of a lot of other people.

All I had to do now was watch how my three arrows changed the mood.

* * *

Several days had passed since I finished laying the groundwork for my strategy, and everyone had completed their tasks. Among the girls in class, the attitude toward the tournament hadn't changed dramatically, but it had definitely changed nonetheless.

"Hey, Yuzu! Has the sport been picked yet?"

"Yeah! I'm going to announce it at the next long homeroom, but we're doing softball!"

"Huh."

"Basketball was popular with the other grades, too, so we did rock-paper-scissors, and I lost. But then softball was our second choice, and I didn't even have to rock-paper-scissors for that one."

"Uh-huh. Gotcha."

If I told you the one asking all the questions was Erika Konno, you could see how much the mood had changed. She'd gone from being totally uninterested in the tournament to actively asking questions about it. Okay, so that "uh-huh" was a sign she was still pretending not to care, but I felt she really was just pretending. This was major progress.

"So who's our pitcher gonna be? Yuki?"

"Uh, I played softball, but I was on third."

"Yeah, but aren't you the only choice?"

And in response to their leader, the other members of the Konno group gradually started to show some interest, too. Some were probably just following her lead, but my guess is that the others were always interested and had just been hiding it because of her. In any case, when the person who normally set the mood changed direction, the group around her immediately changed, too. This was the opposite of the Nakamura incident—when he was absent, everyone started dividing into new factions. When the central figure indicated a clear direction, the group came together.

After that, I could have safely said the girls in the class were excited for the tournament, I think. But while my strategy was partly to thank (along with the work of Hinami, Mizusawa, and Izumi), the cleanest hit surprisingly came from the fact that Izumi was now captain. Just when Erika Konno was starting to show a willingness to participate a bit, Izumi gave her an extra push, and the end result was a kind of synergy.

Also, if I was right that Erika Konno had her eye on Hirabayashi-san for some reason, then it's highly likely that she was being so stubbornly unmotivated because of who was captain. When her friend Izumi took over, that had a big impact. I was so grateful for Izumi's personal growth.

Anyway, all those little factors came together to make a big change in Konno's attitude. Instead of using one hard push to turn everything around, I'd nudged her little by little and ultimately achieved a big result. In that sense, my strategy had the same structure as my general approach to life, and to lots of the games I played. Now I just had to wait for the tournament itself.

* * *

We had three days to go, and school had just let out.

"Yeah, it's safe to say you've passed your assignment."

Hinami was giving me her grade before the big day even arrived.

"Really? I'm already done?"

"Yep."

True enough, in the few days that had passed since I saw her bombarding Izumi with questions, Konno had become totally wrapped up in the tournament. She had an inherent desire to be better than other people, so

I guess once she gave in and started to do something, she felt the need to do it well. In that way, she reminded me of Nakamura.

"I doubt we have anything to worry about at this point…and even if everything goes south, I'd still say you passed after how much you managed to influence Konno."

"Yesss!"

I pumped my fist without a hint of self-consciousness. Man, that was a long assignment. But it was a fun one—it really felt like a game.

"I hope you can stay this positive for the tournament, but for someone as out of shape as you, that's gonna be hard."

"Ouch…"

My spirits fell as Hinami put into words what I'd already faintly sensed myself. She grinned at me with satisfaction.

"Anyway, it was fun to watch nanashi put together a strategy. I meant for this to be a tough one, but you did a surprisingly good job of it."

"Uh, oh, really?"

I was wide open, and the sudden pivot from insults to praise landed a solid hit. *Shit, now what do I do?* I was happy, though; I couldn't help it.

Hinami must have instantly recognized that my guard was down; she smiled with a mature sexiness, parted her soft lips, and hit me with a "Nice work." *Okay, Hinami, now I know you're just trying to embarrass me. I won't give in that easily.*

"So, uh, so what's my next assignment?"

Fighting against her seductive gaze, I changed the subject. She smiled sadistically as I struggled to regain my composure.

"What's the matter?"

"N-nothing. I just asked about my next assignment."

"Is that so?"

"Y-y-yes, it is."

She was intentionally winding me up with her relentless questions. Nope, I'd lost. I could barely get a hit in during this exchange. She really knew how to push my buttons.

Apparently satisfied, she returned to her usual cool attitude.

"Anyway, you're right. Rather than waiting around to see what happens, you'd be better off moving efficiently ahead. I think you should leave Erika Konno behind and go on to your next assignment."

"...Got it."

I nodded, finally calm again. I'd had a break over the past few days as I watched my strategy unfold, so I was ready to go again. *Bring it on!*

"Now then, your assignment for the three days between now and the tournament is..."

"Oh boy..." I braced myself.

"...to devote yourself completely to improving your layup." With the utmost gravity, she announced a majorly disappointing task in the most serious of tones.

"...Seriously?"

She smiled teasingly at my reaction.

"The whole class is excited for the tournament now. It would be a shame not to win, wouldn't it?"

"...Ha-ha."

Hinami's smile was oddly amusing, and I couldn't help laughing a little. Here it was again—her obsession with being number one. The boys' team really had nothing to do with her, but I guess she wanted a double win for our class?

"I'm fairly sure the girls will manage to take first place. My work on the student council hasn't really started yet, so I can focus on this. Having Erika Konno on board now is huge, and so is the fact that Nakamura is back at school. You guys need to get on top of this. Considering who you've got on your team, winning isn't a complete fantasy."

"You think so...?"

"Not that it'll make much difference even if you do improve, but I'd like to shore up that weak point of yours."

"Weak point..."

She was right, but hearing the truth still hurt. I wanted to have a good time at the tournament, but maybe it'd be better if I just didn't play at all.

"But...three days of practice won't change much, will it?" I asked. Hinami wagged her finger at me.

"Listen. You're not going to be practicing every move in basketball, just your layups. If you focus on that, you can wait by the basket for someone to pass you the ball at the right moment and toss it in. It's not a typical position, but that's fine. There probably won't even be real man-to-man defense in the tournament."

I couldn't help smiling at her bizarre but weirdly practical strategy.

"Okay, I get it…but is this really the assignment you want to give me? I mean, everything else has had to do with social stuff."

Hinami smiled smugly.

"What are you talking about? This is going to help on that front, too."

"Really?"

Hinami answered in her usual rational tone. "You can finally join in on conversations with Nakamura's group, but you're still mostly incapable of talking to more than half the kids in our class. I heard Tachibana even forgot your name the other day."

"Uh…"

So my classmates still saw me that way.

"You already have the skills to speak normally with the other guys in class; you just haven't had the opportunity. I know three days is a lot to spend on something completely unrelated to communication skills, but remember this is like taking a shortcut to making conversation opportunities. It's not an entirely inefficient thing to do."

Hinami smiled proudly.

"Um…so you want me to practice layups and find a role to play in the tournament so I can talk with the jocks in class…"

"Basically."

So she wasn't just trying to score a win; she was also thinking about my position in the class. *Hats off to you, Hinami.*

"Plus, you should get some EXP from the new environment this assignment creates."

"…Oh right."

I thought back a couple of days to the incident with Tachibana-kun. He'd joined our conversation for the first time, and I'd gotten so nervous that the whole series of exchanges felt like uncharted territory. It really lit a fire under my butt. By intentionally pushing me out of my comfort zone, she wanted me to collect more EXP on a daily basis.

"This will be a good opportunity, right?"

"Well, now that you've put it like that...yeah."

I had to admit she was right.

"Anyway, I want you to start layup practice after school today... Remember, you're aiming for number one."

"Ha-ha...got it."

Hinami told me about a park between school and the train station where I could use the basketball courts, and with that, my intensive training began. She would stop by after track practice to give me tips and correct my form. And make fun of my horrible coordination.

Seriously, though. She's even found a way turn layup practice into EXP for my ultimate goals—just how logical was she?

5

Sometimes you'll trigger a flag you've been ignoring when you least expect it

Three days had passed since I started practicing my layup, and the sports tournament was here.

We were playing in a typical league, round-robin style, and our class was doing great.

In the gym, I watched as Mizusawa cleanly slipped past the guy defending him and scored a layup.

"Nice one, Takahiro!"

"Thanks!"

He was kicking butt. Teams were free to change up the players on the court for every game, but he'd been in almost all of them. Was he on the basketball team? He looked like he might be, but I had a hard time remembering who played what.

As for me, I still hadn't played a single game. Not much I could do about that. You could tell just by looking at me that I wouldn't be of much use. That said, I knew I'd get out there at some point. According to the tournament rules, everyone in class had to play at least one game. Good thing, since this was a school event. So I'd get my turn eventually...right after this game, in fact.

I was nervous. But I'd also done my best to work on my layups like Hinami had told me, and I wanted to see if my hard work would pay off in a real game. I was especially curious because I hadn't had a chance to play any practice games. My gamer side was rearing its head again.

"Hey!"

"Whoa!"

I whipped my head around, reacting dramatically to the sudden shout. It was Izumi, wearing a summery gym uniform consisting of shorts and a T-shirt that was reflecting the light from the window right into my eyes. Not that I could tear my eyes away from her when she was showing so much skin…

"How's it going over here?" she asked, bouncing over to me. Izumi being Izumi, some other stuff bounced, too.

"Oh, um…we've got three games left including this one, and if we win two of them, I guess we win the whole thing."

"Really? Wow!"

"Yeah…and…," I said, glancing at the court. "It looks like we'll win this game, so we just need one more."

"Nice! You're almost there!"

"Yeah."

In other words, I had to play when the pressure was highest. Glad I practiced.

"Sounds like we might get a double win!"

"Huh? So the girls are…?"

Izumi burst into a grin. "We won our last game, and we've got one more to win the tournament!"

"No way!"

So the girls were set to go, too. Since softball games took longer than basketball games, they were playing knockout style, and the next game would decide everything.

"Yeah, we won the last game in the bottom of the ninth when Erika hit a home run!"

"Konno…hit a home run…?"

I smiled, imagining the scene. Not long ago, she'd been totally apathetic about the tournament, and now she hit a home run? She must have been swinging as hard as she could—talk about being motivated. When a leader goes for it, they really go for it.

"How's it going for you? Did you play yet?"

"Um, not yet… I'm up next," I said hesitantly.

"Ooh, perfect timing! I came over to watch because the game to decide third place in softball is happening before ours."

"O-oh, really…?" I said, even though I wouldn't exactly call the timing "perfect." I mean, I didn't want everyone to see me hanging out under the basket waiting for opportunities to make layups. Personally, I was satisfied with the effort I put in, but it wouldn't exactly look cool. Well, whatever. At least it might make for a good conversation starter. No one was expecting much from me to begin with.

Suddenly, I heard a whistle, and the game was over.

"Okay, one more to go," Mizusawa said, walking breezily over to the normies. He usually acted so mature, but right now he was grinning like a kid and acting extra friendly. The sweat dripping down his chin and neck was glittering in the summer sun like something out of a teen movie.

"Damn, why's he so good-looking…?"

Izumi laughed at my honest comment. "I think Hiro's scored some points for himself at this tournament…," she said, looking to the side with an amused smile. *What?* I followed her gaze and saw Mizusawa in the center of a crowd of girls gushing over his performance.

"…Figures."

Even I thought he was a near-perfect male specimen. The girls must find him irresistible. The gods are unfair.

He looked over at us, waved casually, and headed our way. His smile really was happier and more alive than usual—maybe it was the adrenaline from the game. His giant grin and his short, loose perm were so perfect together that I could almost see beams of light radiating from him. He walked right up to me, switched to a cooler smile, and clapped me on the back.

"Okay, Fumiya, we're gonna win this, right?" he said, looking out over the court. What a dependable guy.

"Uh, right."

I could never imitate his aura by copying his words or actions. It was something abstract that was born from everything he did and his underlying confidence. I guess all I could do was keep working on my expression and posture and tone and stuff like that.

The next game was about to start. The team was Mizusawa, Takei, Tachibana-kun, some guy I didn't really know, and me.

"Okay, everyone! The game is starting!" shouted the other class's captain, who was in charge of this court. A second later, Mizusawa was striding onto the court. He was incredibly energetic for just having played a game. I was only a few seconds behind him. *Okay, let's do this.*

"Go, team!" Izumi yelled, grinning.

I smiled back and walked onto the court.

* * *

Shit. I'm not making any of these layups.

I waited under the basket in a panic. Five minutes had already passed since the game began, and these tournament games lasted only ten minutes. I'd done essentially nothing so far. I'd be in big trouble if I stayed this way. Conversation with the jocks would be out of the question.

Okay, early in the game, Takei had shouted, "It's all you, Farm Boy!" and passed me the ball like he was throwing a Frisbee to a dog, and I'd calmly nailed a perfect layup. Hinami's instructions on the form, steps, and method for assessing distance had paid off.

Mizusawa had shouted, "F-Fumiya?!" in shock, while Takei freaked out and yelled, "Who are you, and what have you done with Farm Boy?!"

Fine, I can understand why Mizusawa reacted that way, but why'd Takei pass me the ball if he was so sure I'd miss the shot? And me being me, I was admittedly smug about all my hard work paying off. So it was going great up until then.

But after that, someone started guarding me. I didn't have the skills or strength to shake him off, and I turned into a waste of court space. I hadn't touched the ball since. On the bright side, an essentially useless player like myself was now occupying one of the opposing team's players, so I wasn't entirely worthless. In that sense, you could say my work had paid off. Maybe?

Plus, the all-important game was turning out to be an even match. Or more accurately—we were losing by three points.

The problem didn't seem to be with our team, despite the fact that

Mizusawa was getting tired. Our opponents were just really damn good. After all, even though Hinami had said there wouldn't be man-to-man defense in the tournament, they'd slapped someone on me the second I made that first layup.

"Got it!" Mizusawa said, intercepting a pass. He sped across the court and released the ball.

"Takei!"

"Nice pass! I'm on it!"

Takei smoothly caught the ball, dribbled dramatically around the guy guarding him, raced over to the basket, and scored with a crazy layup. With his build, speed, and totally unnecessary flair, it almost looked like a dunk. Wow. That was very impressive.

"Whooooooo!" The crowd went wild. A huge grin spread across Takei's face, and he did a double thumbs-up. How is he not embarrassed? I've never seen anyone follow up such a cool move by being that uncool. Never change, Takei.

Someone tossed the ball back onto the court, and we started playing again. Now we were just one point behind. One more basket, and we'd be on top. I think we had about a little over a minute left.

The other team had the ball to start. Their strategy seemed to be just running down the clock. As the five of them tossed the ball back and forth at a healthy pace, they showed no sign of aggressive offense.

Of course—it was the natural strategy, given they were beating us and there wasn't much time on the clock. Some people might call it cowardly, but there was nothing wrong with using the rules to your advantage. They went on passing the ball around the safest route.

And as time dragged on, defeat grew more certain.

Shit. If we don't do something, we'll lose. We were all thinking the same thing when it happened.

Maybe it was a wild instinct, or maybe it was a wild animal's ability to track objects in motion—whatever the case, some sort of animal force seemed to be driving Takei as he darted out like lightning and into the ball's path a couple of steps away from him.

"Nice!" Mizusawa shouted with uncharacteristic excitement.

But the ball slipped out of Takei's hands and bounced across the court. No one was standing in its path. The closest players to it were Takei, the guy guarding me, and me.

"Tch!" My guard glanced at me, clicked his tongue, and ran toward the ball. I couldn't peel myself away from the basket. The ball was now approximately halfway between Takei and the other guy. It was bouncing toward us, so they were probably going to get it.

"Yahhhh!"

But Takei was now a wild animal. Without any regard for his own safety, he hurled himself at the ball and wrapped his arms around it before his opponent had a chance.

"Defense!" the other team's leader shouted. They started racing toward the basket where I was standing.

For the moment, though, I was the only one there.

"Tomozaki!!"

Still sprawled on the ground, Takei called my name—not Farm Boy, but Tomozaki—and passed me the ball. When did my school's sports tournament become the setting of a basketball manga, and how the hell did I end up starring in its climax? Anyway, Takei passed me the ball with all his heart, and I caught it.

We had around ten seconds left. This was truly our last chance.

But I was a little too far away for a layup shot. I dribbled a couple of feet, grabbed the ball in both hands, and got into my layup position. If I missed, we'd lose.

Yup, if I missed, we'd lose.

Lose.

So yeah, of course the pressure would get to me.

"Ngaaaah!"

I might have been putting my all into it, but I'd still practiced my layups for only three days. It was a rush job. I wasn't good enough yet to do it automatically, but how could I think through every single motion in a situation like this?

My feet wouldn't quite cooperate, and that was when one guy from the other team reached the basket.

"Stop him!" one of his teammates screamed in a bloodcurdling voice.

"Ah!"

Panicked, I stumbled over myself and lost my balance. The ball slipped out of my hands and bounced off the ground. Shit.

I struggled to move my tangled feet forward and somehow catch the ball. But I was panicking, so I stumbled again and flew forward onto the ground.

My opponent watched me in shock but kept running toward the ball. I reached for it, and so did he. And then—

Still lying on the ground, I pulled the ball into my armpit with one arm and grabbed the bottom of my opponent's jersey with the other. I-if I could just pull myself up and pass the ball…

Just then, I noticed that everyone, both on and off the court, was staring at the ref. He blew his whistle.

"Uh, red team…!"

Red team. That was us. The ref looked at me.

"Foul…and double dribble, and traveling…!"

Rahhhh!

The crowd erupted for a totally different reason than I had intended.

* * *

I was standing on the side of the court after the game ended.

"Ha-ha-ha… Don't worry about it, man."

Mizusawa gave me a beautiful smile and thumped me on the shoulder.

"G-gimme a break…"

I managed a listless comeback. Izumi giggled awkwardly. And after she'd come over just to watch our game, too.

Takei, who was standing right in front of me, burst out with laughter. "Farm Boy… I've never seen someone break three rules at once!"

He was gripping his stomach and pointing at me, his eyes teary.

"Shut up!" I shouted back, louder than usual because I was so embarrassed. I didn't practice my comebacks for these kinds of situations! A cluster of classmates standing nearby burst into laughter, too. Well, at least I was reaching a wider audience.

Tachibana had been watching and laughing nearby, too, and he pulled himself together and walked over to us.

"Man, that was hilarious!"

"Aw, come on…," I said with melodramatic chagrin so it was clear to him how I felt. He laughed even harder.

"Seriously, though, those guys were good. Not much you could do."

"Yeah," I said, still feeling a little guilty. "Good luck on the last game."

"Leave it to me."

Tachibana grinned, patting my arm. He must be on the basketball team if he was going to be in the crucial final game. Maybe sometimes you can judge a book by its cover.

So if I was talking to the jock Tachibana, did that mean my assignment wasn't a total failure? Uh…

As I was mulling that over, Tachibana sighed and gave me a chill smile.

"Actually, you're surprisingly…"

"…Hmm?"

He was still smiling as he finished the sentence.

"…fun to talk to, Tomoshima-kun!"

"It's Tomozaki."

He still didn't remember my name.

* * *

After two more games between the other teams, the last basketball game of the tournament began. This was the home stretch, and our victory was depending on it.

Since the results would determine who won the whole tournament, the area around the court was packed with spectators. If we won, we'd take first place. If we lost, we'd take second. In the latter case, our opponent for this game wouldn't be the ones who took first—it would be the team we had lost to, thanks to me, in our last game.

"Let's do this!"

Nakamura led the team onto the court.

The team was made up of Tachibana and two other members of the basketball team, plus Mizusawa and Nakamura. It said something about Nakamura's all-around athleticism that he had been chosen for this elite team of the best players in our class even though he was on the soccer team.

As I waited for the game to start, I saw a group of students heading toward us from the baseball field. They were the girls from our class, which meant their tournament must be over. Izumi was leading the pack at a trot, waving at the guys.

"We won the softball tournament!"

She was smiling with heartfelt happiness, but I could also sense her dependability and leadership as the captain. Hinami and Mimimi were behind her, waving and smiling at us. Behind them was Erika Konno, wiping the glittering sweat from her face as she chatted cheerfully with her crew.

As the guys in our class called back to Izumi, she shouted toward the court.

"Shuji! No mercy if you lose!!"

Nakamura scratched his head and sleepily raised his eyebrows, a hint of happiness in his expression.

"I know, I know. I'm on it."

He grinned a powerful, manly grin.

* * *

The final, decisive game was drawing to a close. Nakamura had the ball. Dribbling, he glanced to the left and right, mapping the defense—and then suddenly took off running.

He shook off his defense with pure speed and powerful dribbles, and he was across the court in a flash. He didn't get quite far enough to shoot, though. The other team had made it to the basket first and blocked his path. At the very least, he wouldn't be able to do a layup.

A second later, Nakamura stopped a few steps from the defense and took a shooting position. He was just outside the three-point line.

Realizing what was going on, the defense went for him, but he jumped backward out of their reach. A few seconds remained on the clock. At the peak of his leap, he released the ball.

The ref blew his whistle. This shot was gonna be a buzzer beater.

Under the full attention of the silent spectators and players, the ball traced a slow, graceful arc against the backdrop of the blue, late-summer sky beyond the windows.

And then very quietly, it swished through the basketball hoop.

"Whoooo!"

The final score was twenty-three to eight—we would have won with or without Nakamura's shot. That buzzer beater wasn't deciding a super-close game; it was just kicking them while they were down. We already knew who would win after the first few minutes.

No surprises there. Our opponents in the nail-biter we'd played just before had been the second-place team, and this time, we had even better players on the court. Barring any unforeseen circumstances, we were bound to win. Plus, our opponents this time wouldn't get first place in the tournament no matter what they did, so they probably weren't that motivated. That's reality for you. Still, our victory meant both the guys and girls won the tournament.

"We're number one!!"

Takei hadn't played the last game, despite being the captain, but he still pointed to the ceiling and raised a warlike shout as our leader. Nakamura and Mizusawa followed suit and pointed at the ceiling, too, smiling happily. Most of the girls from our class were crowded around, and everyone was shouting and cheering. Hinami, Mimimi, and Tama-chan had their arms around one another's shoulders. Tama-chan had to stand on her tiptoes.

I glanced at Erika Konno. Her smile was more reserved, but I could tell she was happy. When Izumi threw her arms around Konno's neck with a huge grin, Konno ruffled her hair good-naturedly.

Wow. Everyone seemed to be having fun. I felt like the whole class had come together as one. The old me never would have done it, but I joined the crowd and tried cheering a little myself. I wasn't sure, but it didn't feel like a very good fit for me. Well, that's life. Not everyone has fun in the same way.

"Nice job!"

Izumi pulled away from Konno and gave everyone a captain-like word of congratulations.

"You guys won, too, right? Our class rules," Nakamura said casually.

"We sure do!"

Izumi raised one hand to about head height. What was she doing? As I was puzzling over this, Nakamura raised his hand, too, and they met with a slap in midair against the sun. Oh, a high five. I'd been watching, but I had no idea that was coming. Those two really did think alike. Or was I just clueless about normie culture? That was probably it.

I looked over at Takei and noticed he was staring sorrowfully at his own palm. *I get you, man. You're captain, after all.* Normally, the two captains would do the high five here. Poor Takei.

The tournament over, we joined the closing ceremony and then went back to our classroom. By the way, the closing ceremony included a rousing speech from our new student council president, Hinami. Watching her, I thought about how each of us had our role to play.

* * *

A few hours later, Hinami, Mizusawa, Takei, Mimimi, and I were heading to the train station from school, and we were peering around the corner from the shadows of a building. A couple was walking side by side down the nearly empty street—Izumi and Nakamura.

Yes, they were walking home from school together, and we were tailing them.

"Well, well, I wonder what's going to happen!" Mimimi said, clearly enjoying this.

"Yeah, me too," I said, thinking back to what had happened after the tournament.

The whole class had been treated to ice cream as a reward for taking first place. Apparently, Hinami had conspired with Kawamura-sensei to buy it using student council funds. Wait, is that allowed? Not that I mind.

The celebration went on for a couple of hours, until it was time to go home.

Finally, Izumi took action.

She walked up to Nakamura while he was talking to Mizusawa and Takei and abruptly made a proposition.

"Shuji… Wanna walk home together?"

Her boldness—her strength to do whatever she put her mind to—had seemed to define her lately. Nakamura gave her a short "Sure, whatever," which was his way of agreeing.

The rest of us, who had been listening from nearby, made comments like, "Oh, okay, see you guys tomorrow," and started casually letting them know they could do what they wanted. As soon as they left, we all huddled and unanimously agreed we had to tail them. And here we were.

"What are they gonna do?!" Hinami whispered.

"This has got to be it. We had a double victory at the tournament, and Yuzu even brought Shuji back to school with the power of love," Mizusawa said.

"What are you talking about?" Mimimi asked, frowning.

"Oh…a lot happened while you were fooling around with Tama," Mizusawa answered.

"What's that supposed to mean?! Details! Gimme the rundown!"

We filled her in on the events of the past couple weeks as we kept following Izumi and Nakamura. Pretty soon, they veered off the usual route home. We couldn't figure out why. Which meant…?

Mimimi leaned forward, eyes sparkling. "Ooh, where are they going?"

"Hey, get back, Mimimi! They'll see you," Hinami said, pulling her back with an exasperated smile.

"I knew we shouldn't have brought her along…," Mizusawa joked.

"Well, aren't you a sassmaster today? If you're nitpicky about everything, you'll never get a girlfriend!"

"Ha-ha-ha. I think girls like me fine."

"Really now? And yet you're still single, Takahiro!"

"Shut up. I just don't do things halfway. Anyway, look who's talking. Where's your boyfriend?"

"I don't need one. I have Tama! Right, Tomozaki?"

"Wh-why are you asking me?"

While we were busy joking around, the two lovebirds had headed for an empty park.

"Oh shit! It's getting real!"

Takei managed not to shout while he was jumping around excitedly, but we still had to shush him for being way too loud. He got all depressed and looked down with apologetic, silent grief. *C-come on, man, don't get depressed!*

Anyway, I recognized the park they'd walked into. It was the same place I'd been practicing layups. Was Nakamura going for a bittersweet romantic scene? Maybe he'd say something like *If I can make this shot, be my girlfriend!* Or maybe not.

We followed them into the park, whispering excitedly and sticking to the trees around the edge, where we'd have a view of the central area. The two of them sat down next to each other on a bench facing the entrance.

"Damn, they're looking this way. We can't get any closer." Mizusawa sounded disappointed.

"…Wait," I said as he made a move to put down his school bag.

"Huh?" He looked at me expectantly as I nodded and pointed across the path.

"There's another entrance over there. If we go to that side, we can get a lot closer."

"No way!"

"Yeah."

I'd have never guessed my layup practice would pay off in this way, but I had a fairly good sense of the park's layout. I gave a thumbs-up, and Mimimi thumped my back and whispered, "Nice!" It hurt, which meant she was in a good mood.

We crept around the park, went through the other entrance, and stealthily approached. We ended up in the shadow of an equipment shed a couple of yards from the bench, and if we strained our ears, we could just make out what they were saying. After a quick glance at one another, we focused on eavesdropping.

"...Right! And then Aoi took over as pitcher for the rest of the game!"

Izumi was talking, and she'd just revealed something new to me. I didn't know Hinami had pitched the end of the winning game. I looked at her, and she gave me a goofy *You got me!* smile. As always, her perfect-heroine expressions made you want to laugh.

"Ha-ha-ha. She's always so pushy, huh?"

"Well, thanks to her, we won!"

I almost burst out laughing at Nakamura's refreshing description of Hinami. He was right; if someone asked me whether she was pushy, I'd have to say yes. Not only was she the student council president and the class leader, but she was also the pitcher in the final game of the tournament? That she managed to do it without being obnoxious was a testament to her well-balanced personality. Of course, from my perspective, she was nothing *but* obnoxious.

"You didn't do so bad yourself, huh?" Nakamura said bluntly. We looked at one another and sniggered. Even now he was playing it cool.

"Um...," Izumi answered haltingly. "Uh, yeah. I guess."

"Hmm..."

"Hey, that didn't sound like you."

Nakamura gave a sudden, offhand smile. "What's that supposed to mean? What am I supposed to sound like?"

"Uh, um...meaner?"

"Hey, jerk!"

With that, Nakamura clamped his hand on the top of Izumi's head.

"Ow, ow, ow!"

"Are you saying I'm mean?"

Izumi grabbed Nakamura's arm with both hands, but he didn't let go. She was squealing but not really trying to push him off. And after a little while of that...

"So you wanna go out with me?"

"Eeeek?!"

Izumi yelped at Nakamura's abrupt question, and I almost did, too.

I clapped both hands over my mouth, and when I had calmed down, I realized everyone aside from Takei had their hands over their mouths, too. Takei's mouth was covered by Hinami's hand. Huh? ...Had she instantly recognized the danger and covered hers and his at the same time? If so, it was an excellent decision.

Anyway, what the heck just happened? Things went from zero to a hundred in about one second. They'd been dragging along forever, and now all of a sudden, they were leaps and bounds ahead of what any of us expected. On the other hand, it seemed in character for Nakamura.

He went on, as cool and blunt as ever.

"What was that noise? You sound ridiculous."

"H-hey, no, I don't!"

"Well, what's your answer?" he said irritably.

Seriously, what was his deal? He took forever to tell her how he felt, then once he did, he acted all cocky and superior about it. Or was it just a top-tier thing? Geez, dude.

"Um...when you say 'go out'..."

"Huh? I mean, nothing will change, really."

"R-right..."

Izumi looked down silently for a minute. I couldn't see her face, but I could imagine how red it must be. The silence continued. Nakamura was sitting with his knees spread, looking casually away from her. How did he emit such a powerful aura of unconcern that I could read it from behind?

Finally, Izumi turned to face him.

"...Yes, I'd like to. Because I like you, too."

Her voice was strong and grounded, but I could make out an excited heat in it, too. We crouched there in the shade of the equipment shed, our hands still over our mouths, looking at one another with satisfaction.

"...Okay, then."

Maybe to hide his shyness, Nakamura stood up and started walking toward the main park entrance. "Wait!" Izumi shouted. He turned toward her. A second before he did, Hinami and Mizusawa pulled us behind the shed. *G-good job, guys.*

"What?"

Hiding behind the shed, we could only hear them.

"It's just...I said I liked you, *too*...but you never actually said how you felt. And I don't want to put words in your mouth or anything..."

She sounded faintly nervous, but I could tell she was trying very hard to sound extremely nonchalant.

"...Huh? What are you talking about?"

Nakamura was trying to stay blunt, but I also thought I could hear his cool facade breaking down, little by little. Finally, we heard the sound of something like sand or gravel crunching underfoot. I didn't know who it was.

"I just...want to know."

Izumi's voice was so earnest, like she had gathered all her strength to get the words out.

Silence.

The wind blew, fluttering Mimimi's and Hinami's hair. There was a dry sound like falling leaves scuttling across the ground.

The wind stopped. I heard that gravel sound again.

"I like you, too."

The summer heat had died down now, replaced by the cool, pleasant air of late September.

"I'm glad."

Izumi's reply was soft and short, but overflowing with a happy sweetness. Behind the shed, we looked at one another wide-eyed, breath held and hands still over our mouths. Then we all nodded, although I had no idea what it was supposed to mean.

"Let's get going."

"...Okay!"

After Izumi's short, satisfied answer, we heard two sets of footsteps retreating. We stayed there for a moment as their lingering happiness wafted through the park.

"They're gone...!"

Mimimi looked around at us impatiently. Hinami poked her head out from behind the shed, surveyed the scene, then looked back at us and nodded. All clear. We all let out our breath.

"Sh-Shuji! Way to go, dude!" Takei gushed as soon as he was released, although his voice was a little tight. Hinami looked at him and smiled.

"Yeah, it sure took them long enough!"

Her tone conveyed a mixture of exasperation, amusement, and affection. I didn't want to think about how much of it was her acting. Scary.

"Young love in bloom before our eyes! I've gotta keep up!"

Mimimi, who for some reason was taking a competitive approach to the situation, pounded my back as I crouched in the shadows. Ouch!

"Hey, that hurts! …But yeah, guess the drama's over."

I sighed. Maybe life wasn't so bad after all if there were happy endings like this. This game did have its good points.

Suddenly, I heard someone laughing behind me.

"…To their long and happy life together!" I could see a touch of chagrin in Mizusawa's smile as he joked, but he still looked like he was having the most fun of any of us.

* * *

"So actually…we're dating now."

The next morning in class, Izumi announced her news, her face beet red. Nakamura was standing next to her.

"What?! Seriously?! Congratulations!"

Following Hinami's lead, we all pretended we had no idea what had happened the day before. Her performance was perfect, of course.

"Who said something first?! Nakamu?!"

"I don't think Shuji has it in him!"

Mimimi and Mizusawa joined in with equally perfect, teasing performances.

"Shut up. Who cares anyway?"

Nakamura was being as cocky as ever. He could be so annoying.

"Wow, I never would have expected this!"

"Y-yeah! Congratulations, Izumi and Nakamura!"

While everyone else was busy being smooth, Takei and I offered our clumsy reactions. Cut us some slack, okay? At least it wasn't enough for them to guess we'd seen the whole thing.

"Thanks!"

"Enough already. It's not like anything's gonna change."

While Izumi answered with honest appreciation, Nakamura abruptly tried to change the subject, probably out of embarrassment. They were definitely an odd couple, but in my opinion, that made them just right for each other.

Soon, the whole class knew and started congratulating the new couple. The general mood had been pushing for them to get together, so some people were even like, "Took you long enough!"

As I was thinking the other day, the whole thing ended without anything bad happening to anyone. Everyone was satisfied, and the mood was good. Life would go on as usual. And everyone lived happily ever after—

—or not. I was about to learn that the game of life wasn't quite that sweet.

6

A happy ending doesn't mean this game is over

I first sensed something was off the Monday after Izumi and Nakamura started dating.

A loud clatter came from the front of the classroom.

"Oh, sorry!"

A pencil case had fallen onto the floor, the contents scattering everywhere. The students sitting nearby stopped the rolling erasers with their feet. Someone must have carelessly bumped into the case, knocking it off the desk and onto the floor, and quickly apologized.

There was nothing so unusual about that. It happened relatively often. What made me uneasy was the identity of the student apologizing, and the person they were apologizing to.

The one apologizing was Erika Konno.

The one being apologized to was Hirabayashi-san.

Erika Konno had knocked Hirabayashi-san's pencil case onto the floor and offered a quick "sorry!" Then she headed over to her usual spot by the window and started chatting with her crew instead of helping pick up the pencils. That wasn't too surprising from her.

Honestly, it was kind of uncomfortable. But she *had* apologized, and it wasn't a big enough deal to deserve criticism. After all, the students sitting near Hirabayashi-san helped pick up the pencils and erasers, so everything was cleaned up quickly. I bet most people thought to themselves, *Oh, Erika Konno is acting like she runs the world again*, and stopped at that. Just another day in our class.

But that impression quickly changed.

Because it didn't stop.

Of course, I didn't mean that Erika Konno kept knocking Hirabayashi-san's pencil case onto the ground. It was a string of little things. For example, when one member of Konno's group and Hirabayashi-san were both in charge of class chores, Konno made Hirabayashi-san do all the work, just as she'd forced her to become captain. Another time, during break, a paper airplane Konno had made using one of her groupies' papers just *happened* to hit Hirabayashi-san on the head. And whenever she walked near Hirabayashi-san's desk, she just *happened* to kick the leg.

If you looked at the incidents individually, you might assume Erika Konno was just in a bad mood that day. But this string of little incidents was all piling up on Hirabayashi-san.

After about a week of this, I and most of the other students had noticed she was doing it on purpose. And she was doing it to be mean. Erika Konno's actions were turning the classroom into an uncomfortable place to be, and everybody, probably including those in her group, wanted it to end as quickly as possible.

But if you really wanted to, you could write off each mean little thing she did as a coincidence. That's what made it so hard to tell her to stop. We were starting to assume her actions were inevitable, and they were suffocating the class.

* * *

"Hey, Tomozaki."

Izumi started up a conversation one day after school.

"Uh, what's up?"

I turned toward her. She was peering at me intensely.

"...Izumi?" I asked. She seemed to be having a hard time saying what she wanted to say.

"It's about Erika..."

"Oh..."

She probably meant the situation with Konno and Hirabayashi-san.

"She's doing all that stuff on purpose, isn't she?"

"Yeah, I think so..."

Konno was pretending these were all accidents with no deeper meaning, but it was actually harassment. Anyone watching could see what she wanted to do.

Izumi lowered her eyes and bit her lip before looking up at me again.

"I think..."

"...What?"

She scratched her pointer finger with her fingernail.

"I really shouldn't be saying this, but..."

"Yeah?"

She gave me a determined look. "I think it's because of me." She bit her lip again.

"...Uh..."

I couldn't contradict her. Hirabayashi-san had been a kind of target for Erika Konno in the past, too. But why had it escalated lately? I could think of only one answer. In other words...

"...You think it's because you're dating Nakamura?"

Izumi nodded.

"I mean, look at the timing. Erika was upset that we got together, but she couldn't take it out on me or Shuji because that would be too obvious. It makes perfect sense."

"Could be."

There was no way to prove it. But when we had the strategy meeting for the barbecue trip at my house, someone had mentioned that Erika Konno was annoyed that Izumi and Nakamura were getting along so well. It would be a reason for her to be harassing Hirabayashi-san. And if we were right, well, she sure was selfish. It kinda pissed me off.

"But if that's the case, I probably shouldn't say anything to Erika, right?"

As soon as she said it, I realized she was right. I nodded. "Yeah..."

She looked down, dejected.

"...It could be risky," I added.

If she accidentally poked at Konno's wound, the situation could get worse. I didn't say that out loud, but Izumi knew it. My guess was that she'd been seriously considering what she could do to help Hirabayashi-san. But she'd realized she was the one person who absolutely shouldn't take the simplest route, which would be to say something directly to Konno.

We weren't certain Izumi was the reason behind Erika Konno's harassment. But as long as we couldn't fully rule out the possibility, it would be as good as impossible for her to do anything.

"Yeah… Well, thanks."

"No problem," I said gloomily.

"…Also, remember when we were talking about why she's picking on Hirabayashi-san in particular?" Izumi continued quietly.

"Yeah."

"I've been watching the situation this past week, and I think I know the answer."

Her face clouded over. I had an idea what she was going to say. Actually, I think the whole class was starting to guess what the issue was. So I put it into words.

"It's because Hirabayashi-san would never say anything back, isn't it?"

She nodded.

"Yeah… I think she's just an easy target."

"…That's what I thought."

Hirabayashi-san didn't fight back. Erika Konno knew that, and that's why she chose her to pick on. It was incredibly obvious what she was doing, but there were limits to how open she could be about it. That made it all the more obvious that Erika Konno was guilty. It was also a reminder of how random and unfair this game of life could be.

Izumi looked at the clock and slung her bag over her shoulder.

"Um…I've gotta get going."

"Okay… See you later."

"See you later!" she said, clearly making an effort to sound cheerful, and headed off to team practice.

* * *

After Izumi left, I headed to Sewing Room #2 for my after-school meeting with Hinami. I brought up what we'd been talking about in class, and Hinami agreed.

"I think so, too. It started right after those two started dating, didn't it?"

"That must be it."

Hinami nodded.

"She's upset with the two of them, but attacking Yuzu would make her look really bad. The most logical conclusion is that she's taking it out on Hirabayashi-san… She would do that," Hinami said, not hiding her own irritation.

"Huh…"

"Well, we have no proof…but I can say one thing. Yuzu shouldn't say anything to Konno about it."

I was surprised to hear her say the exact same thing we'd been talking about, like she could read our minds.

"…So you think so, too, huh?"

"Uh-huh. Yuzu probably wants to do something right about now, doesn't she?" she said with concern.

"Yeah… How did you guess?"

"I've just been paying attention to her," Hinami said flatly. "But it would be dangerous for her to do anything."

"Yeah…I agree."

Ugh, this was such a headache. Hinami thought silently for a minute, then went on.

"Honestly…as long as Konno doesn't do anything dramatic, there's not much the rest of us can do."

"Because she'll say it's all just coincidence?"

Hinami nodded.

"Right now, it's too minor. The biggest thing she's done so far is probably knocking her pencil case off her desk, right? If she was constantly doing things on that level, it would be one thing, but pointing to all these little incidents and making a big fuss about harassment wouldn't lead to any real solution. She could just play innocent, and then we'd be stuck.

With that approach, she might stop temporarily, but Hirabayashi-san's position in the class would worsen over the long term."

"You're probably right."

I nodded. She seemed correct anyway. We couldn't just think about a short-term solution to the harassment—we had to think about how this would affect Hirabayashi-san in the future.

"...But what do we do?" I asked.

"Right now there's not much we *can* do. Unless she starts something on a bigger scale, our best option is probably to just keep an eye on the situation so it doesn't get any worse."

"...Hmm," I said weakly. I thought back to the idea that had crossed my mind during my conversation with Izumi. This was completely unfair. Which meant...

"Is life really such a great game?" I couldn't help asking Hinami.

"...What do you mean?"

She gave me a penetrating look, and I thought I glimpsed a hint of sadness in her eyes. But maybe she was only sad because I was asking that question.

"I mean, this is basically just bad RNG. This came out of nowhere—it's weird, isn't it? What's so great about that kind of game?"

It was tough to talk about a game I'd come to like in these terms, but I figured I'd better tell Hinami what was on my mind. I was having fun now, and I liked all the cool new scenes I was seeing. But if someone could get hit with something like this for no good reason, wasn't that evidence that the game still had bugs?

Hinami shook her head slowly.

"It didn't come out of nowhere."

"...What are you talking about?"

I waited defensively for her to explain. She ticked off the points on her fingers as she spoke, like a teacher talking to a student.

"Erika Konno liked Nakamura, and so did Yuzu. Nakamura got into a fight with his mom. And Yuzu was the one who saved him from that fight."

She smoothly summarized the recent events.

"Because Yuzu saved him, Nakamura was able to participate in the sports tournament. And because of your assignment, Erika Konno and her followers were invested, too. Thanks to those two factors, both the guys and the girls won the tournament. And because of the victory, Yuzu and Nakamura started dating… Plus, Hirabayashi-san is just a timid person."

Hinami paused for a moment, evidently having finished her list.

"Individually, none of those factors seem important. But when you line them all up, they fall just like dominoes until they reach the last and biggest domino: Erika Konno's harassment. That's not just RNG. Each piece of the story leads to the next, and altogether, they make an outstanding explanation. There's nothing especially random about it. In a sense, it's inevitable."

Her argument wasn't unconvincing. Now that she mentioned it, the harassment was less a momentary whim of Erika Konno's and more the result of several things pointing in the same direction. In that sense, I couldn't say it was random. Maybe it was too soon to trash this game for being unfair.

But something about Hinami's phrasing rubbed me the wrong way.

"Inevitable, really? …Don't you feel bad for Hirabayashi-san? Are you saying we should just leave her?"

Hinami nodded without batting an eye. "Yes, that's what I'm saying."

"Hinami…"

Her expression didn't change.

"Plus…for now, I don't think there's any need to rescue her."

"Huh?" I said before I could stop myself. Why would she say something that?

"I mean, this level of harassment isn't like bullying. The victim can resolve it herself, right? Hirabayashi-san just doesn't have the will to do it. So there's a reason for that, too."

She delivered her explanation like it was the most obvious thing in the world.

"Okay, Hinami—" Naturally, I was getting mad. "Now you're going too far."

Hinami stared at me, expressionless, then quietly replied, "Sorry if I offended you. But as far as I can see, Hirabayashi-san has no interest in fixing the situation herself. If she took some initiative, she could absolutely resolve it. Hirabayashi-san herself is one of the factors motivating Konno."

"She's not— It's..."

Unable to continue, I sat silently for a moment. Izumi and I had talked about the same thing. Like Hinami said, she was being targeted because she didn't fight back. But that didn't mean Hirabayashi-san was doing anything she shouldn't.

"...But Konno's using that to make a target out of her. That's just wrong."

Hinami shook her head.

"I agree that what Erika Konno is doing is pretty low. She's in the wrong here, no question. But didn't you say yourself that gamers grab the controller and forge a path forward? The same goes in life, right?"

"Yes, but..."

"Listen. I agree with you. Not everyone has to be a gamer, sure, but I think our way is the right way. It's how I want to live, at least. And I think it's how you do, too."

"...I guess so," I answered noncommittally, but I nodded. We felt differently about whether to take a player's or a character's perspective, but we shared a belief that one should hold the controller in this fight. When a wall of rules stood in our way, we used critical thinking and experimentation to get results through our own efforts. We never let go of the controller. That was the essential stance of a gamer.

"Right now, Hirabayashi-san isn't picking up the controller. Right?"

"Maybe not...but still..."

No, she probably wasn't trying to be a gamer. She wasn't taking any action or trying any trial and error to change her reality. She appeared to simply accept her daily harassment as inevitable.

"But she's still the victim here," I said.

Hinami nodded.

"Of course. That's why we're even discussing whether or not we should help her. If I see a gamer who's giving their all to advance but failing to resolve a problem, I want to jump in and help. But if she isn't trying to help herself, then there's no need for someone else to reach out a hand. Of course, if the situation deteriorates, I'm planning to step in. All I'm saying is that right now, we're not at the point where I'm definitely going to get involved."

Her words struck me as colder than usual, but maybe they only sounded so cold because I thought the situation deserved more. Yes, this was more serious than usual, but the core of her message hadn't changed in the least.

"I understand what you're trying to say." As always, there was nothing seriously wrong with her argument. "There's nothing compelling you to help her," I went on.

"Right. Just because I *can* help her doesn't mean I *have* to."

"...I see."

In that case, it wouldn't work to try to force Hinami to do something. If I wanted to change the current situation, I'd have to do it myself.

As I sat there looking down and thinking about what I could do, Hinami shot me an exasperated look.

"Let me guess... You're planning to do something, aren't you?"

"Umm...well, if there's anything I can do, then yeah."

Hinami sighed at my honest answer.

"Not long ago I was thinking about how Mizusawa was rubbing off on you, and now it seems like Yuzu's getting to you, too..."

She pressed her temples with frustration.

"No...I'm not trying to be like her."

Even as I said it, though, I realized something. I wasn't especially close with Hirabayashi-san, and heroism wasn't part of my nature. Far from it—I'd never even considered trying to stop the bullying I saw in class before. Now here I was, wanting to do everything I could to help. I didn't know what had caused this internal change, but I suspected Izumi's habit of trying to help other people had played a big role.

Hinami looked at me gravely.

"Well, either way, if you're going to step in, really think it through so you don't make everything worse. You can take a break from assignments for a while. Focus on that instead."

"U-understood."

"Let's just say that that's your assignment: Don't make things worse. The point is, you need to carefully consider how to act before you do anything."

"...Okay."

"For now, I think you'll be best off just observing the situation."

"Observing, huh?"

It didn't sit well with me, but I couldn't think of any practical strategies just yet, so even if I wanted to act now, her suggestion was my only option.

With that, our meeting came to an end.

* * *

The next morning, Hinami and I didn't talk much at our meeting, so we ended earlier than usual. When I got to our classroom, Izumi and Hirabayashi-san were having a chat. Given everything else that had been going on, this probably meant something. Was Izumi working on some kind of plan?

I was curious, so I deliberately took a path to my seat that brought me within eavesdropping distance.

"So you found your desk there this morning?"

"Yeah... I think they did it after school. I mean, I can just put it back..."

"Yes, but..."

They must be talking about Erika Konno's harassment—about the things only Hirabayashi-san herself knew.

I had a guess as to what Izumi was trying to do.

She couldn't negotiate with Erika Konno directly, and there wasn't enough evidence to get an adult involved. Still, she was getting all the information she could from Hirabayashi-san to figure out how she might be able to help. Izumi's kindness was quiet but strong.

"Okay...so they do that stuff if you go home early."

"...Yes, I think so."

Izumi kept glancing at the clock as she talked to Hirabayashi-san with a serious look on her face. Erika Konno hadn't gotten to class yet.

A few minutes later, she checked the clock one more time, then waved at Hirabayashi-san with a smile and walked up to the front of the class where Erika Konno's group was hanging out. A minute or two after that, the queen herself made her entrance and headed for the windows by the front of the class, taking an intentional detour to kick Hirabayashi-san's desk on her way. Then she started talking with her clique.

I spent the rest of the day furtively observing the situation, and I noticed something. During breaks, when Erika Konno went to the bathroom or when Izumi got back to our main classroom before Konno, and after school, when Izumi was getting ready for practice and Konno left before her—in other words, every spare moment that Erika Konno wasn't around—Izumi would go over to Hirabayashi-san and talk to her for a minute or two. She did it again and again from morning until the end of the school day.

She seemed to be working steadily to help solve the problem, even if she couldn't do much, and even if she was on her own.

If she could do that, then what should I do?

* * *

It was break time after first period the next day. As soon as class ended, I turned to Izumi.

"Um, Izumi…"

The day before, after watching her working so hard to help, I'd gone back home and spent a long time thinking in my room. Eventually, I'd hit on something that seemed doable for me.

"What?" She looked at me blankly.

"Uh…" I searched for the words that would let me do what I'd decided on. "Is Hirabayashi-san okay?"

She blinked at me in surprise. "What do you mean, 'okay'?"

"It's just…you were talking to her a lot yesterday."

"Oh, that's what you meant!"

"I was worried about her, so if there's any way I can help, I'd like to."

If I couldn't help Hirabayashi-san directly, I at least wanted to help Izumi. And if I still couldn't do anything there, I at least wanted to talk to Izumi and let her know I was behind her. After all, I was her *Atafami* mentor. When an apprentice is in trouble, the mentor's gotta come to the rescue, right? I mean, we *want* to help.

Izumi looked at me gloomily.

"Well, actually…"

"What's up?"

She lowered her voice. "I think Erika's doing more to her in secret."

"…Really?" I was surprised to hear such bad news. "Like what?"

Izumi looked down at the mechanical pencil in her hand.

"Well, according to Hirabayashi-san…most of her pencil leads have been broken, and her pens won't write even though they have ink in them—things like that."

"Th-that's…"

Erika Konno had to be responsible. Her strategy was relentless. She could say the pencil leads broke when the pencil case fell the other day, and for the pens, she could write them off as bad luck. That would be the end of the discussion. She was probably keeping the harassment at a low level on purpose. What set these latest acts apart was that they caused physical damage.

"If her stuff's getting broken, that's pretty bad."

"…Yeah."

She would have to buy replacements, which meant this was literally costing her money.

"But there's still no evidence, right?"

Izumi gave a frustrated nod.

"Also, I don't think the guys know about this…but for some reason, a new LINE group was created for the girls in our class…"

"Really?"

I didn't even know those existed. Was there a group for the entire class? If so, I wasn't part of it.

"Yeah, and Hirabayashi-san is the only one who isn't in it." Izumi frowned.

"Who made that group?"

"Yumi, but I think Erika told her to do it. She's part of our group."

"Huh..."

Yeah, she was sly, all right. None of the incidents seemed like a big deal on their own, but this constant stream could definitely become a heavy weight. Hopefully, Izumi's soothing, ordinary little chats were bolstering Hirabayashi-san's spirits a little.

"At the very least, we've gotta do something about the damage to her stuff..."

"Yeah..."

I glanced up and noticed that the harassment seemed to be going on even at this very moment. Hirabayashi-san was in the bathroom or something, and while she was gone, Konno and her groupies had set up camp around her desk instead of by the window as usual. Granted, one of the group did sit near Hirabayashi-san, so if anyone confronted them, they could just argue back that they were at their friend's desk.

As I watched them, Hirabayashi-san walked into the classroom from the hallway. Obviously, though, she couldn't sit at her desk. She also couldn't protest the fact that they'd occupied her space.

She stood by the door for a few minutes, took a breath, let it out, and went back into the hallway.

"..."

I couldn't take it anymore. I started to think about how I could shift the mood right now. Maybe if I yelled at Erika Konno like I did before in the old principal's office, then something would change. Or maybe I could manipulate the group using the skills I had learned, since I'd been observing and thinking about it lately.

Just as I was going through each of my assets and reflecting on what I should do, someone else beat me to it.

"Hey, Konno!"

A voice rang out, pure and clear, through the classroom.

Everyone turned to look at the person who had yelled, and Konno especially was furious. I turned in the same direction and blinked in shock. The person standing there was...

* * *

...Tama-chan.

Tama-chan might have been tiny, but her gaze did not waver.

"Haven't you taken this far enough? Just cut it out! This is stupid!"

She pointed accusingly at Konno as she called her out.

Everyone had noticed what was going on, but no one had said anything, either because they thought nothing would change or because they were scared. But not Tama-chan. She struck the problem at its source, right there in front of everyone, with her unvarnished, decisive, direct words.

I couldn't take my eyes off her.

As for Konno—if looks could kill, Tama-chan would be dead.

"What are you talking about?"

She was still playing innocent. But Tama-chan didn't bend.

"Oh, come on! You lost Nakamura, and now you're taking it out on someone else! It's ridiculous!"

Tama-chan was unearthing the core of the problem hidden by Konno's malice, and the atmosphere in the classroom froze.

"Hmph..." Konno looked Tama-chan up and down appraisingly. "Gotcha."

She hopped down from Hirabayashi-san's desk and started making her way to Tama-chan. Her eyes were full of blatant spite, hostility, and vengefulness. Still, she took her time, reminding the rest of us that she didn't *really* care.

She walked right up to Tama-chan, stared her in the eye for a minute, and then smiled triumphantly and a little mockingly. She placed her hand on Tama-chan's shoulder.

"You're shaking, Hanabi."

"Shut up!"

Tama-chan sounded rattled. She shook Konno's hand off roughly, and then Konno pressed her wrist and moaned dramatically, staring down at Tama-chan.

"Owww!" I could see the fury deep in her eyes.

"H-hey, I barely touched you…"

For the first time, Tama-chan let her anxiety show. Konno snorted.

"You hit first," she said. Then she walked over to her usual spot by the window, her crew trailing behind her. An uneasy murmur rippled through the class.

That was when I realized something.

The line of dominoes hadn't finished falling yet.

At this very moment, another one was about to hit the ground.

And when it did, this was going to get even worse than before.

* * *

A loud clatter echoed from the front of the classroom.

"Oh, I'm sooo sorry!"

The mocking, overly innocent voice belonged to Konno. She didn't bother to look at the fallen pencil case as she joined her clique. An uncomfortable tension washed over the class, and it felt like the original malicious act was being repeated all over again. But one thing was very different this time.

I bit my lip as I turned in the direction of the clatter. I think that in some corner of my mind, I had been expecting and fearing this.

The pencil case didn't belong to Hirabayashi-san. It belonged to Tama-chan.

The quiet conversations in the class got a little louder as that dull discomfort hit us. Erika Konno's intentions were all too clear. This was a cruel act, a small one that foretold a hundred more to come.

The target of her malice had just shifted.

This new reality seemed to sting my skin as I walked toward Tama-chan's desk to help her pick up the scattered pencils and erasers. When I glanced around, I saw that Hinami and Mimimi were about to do the same. Just then, it happened again.

* * *

"Konno!"

The same clear, powerful voice called her out for a second time.

I felt like time stood still as my eyes drifted toward her. Hinami, Mimimi, and I all stopped in our tracks. Tama-chan was glaring at Konno's back and howling.

"You did that on purpose!"

There was nothing roundabout or evasive about her words. She went straight to the heart of the matter.

"What? What makes you so sure? Stop assuming things!"

"I'm not assuming!"

"I mean, I did apologize. It's just a pencil case; chill out."

"So what if you apologized? That's not the point!"

"What, then? You gonna hit me again?"

"No, I…! I didn't hit you!"

Ignoring this last protest, Konno went back to chatting with her clique. Tama-chan stared at her for a while, but she eventually gave up and looked away. As she squatted down and began picking up her pencils, I started walking toward her again.

Mimimi jogged over and got there first, followed by me and Hinami, and the four of us gathered up the pencils.

Mimimi gave Tama-chan a serious look. "You didn't do anything wrong," she said with warm encouragement.

"…Yeah." Tama-chan smiled.

"Um…are you okay?"

"…Yeah, I'm fine."

I never knew what to say in situations like this, so I ended up asking a vague question. But Tama-chan gave me a little smile, too.

"Hanabi can handle it," Hinami added.

"Aoi…thank you."

"I…I'll do something."

"…Aoi?"

Seeming to have made her mind up about something, Hinami nodded at Tama-chan.

* * *

The situation changed noticeably after that.

Every time Konno walked somewhere, she kicked Tama-chan's desk instead of Hirabayashi-san's. Tama-chan's mechanical pencil leads and ballpoint pens were broken one after the next. I started to hear Konno's group trash-talking her on a regular basis.

As usual, Erika Konno's foul mood was the single cause of this cruel behavior. Every day, at least once or twice, she or her clique did something to Tama-chan. But there was one big difference compared with when they'd been harassing Hirabayashi-san.

"Konno! You kicked my desk again!"

Every time they did something to her, Tama-chan loudly pointed it out. She stubbornly resisted and refused to break.

Whereas Hirabayashi-san had quietly let everything go, Tama-chan didn't overlook a single offense. She called out Konno every time. Her strong reactions were almost extreme, but that strength felt unstable to me, as if it could collapse at any moment.

Erika Konno never took the bait.

"What are you talking about? It was an accident. Stop accusing me when I didn't do anything to you."

"An accident, huh? You did the exact same thing yesterday!"

"Did you forget you attacked me the other day?"

"No...that was...an accident..."

"What? No, *this* was an accident. You hit me on purpose."

After that hateful accusation, she just ignored Tama-chan's protests of innocence and walked over to her clique.

"Hey, I'm still talking..."

"Now, now, Hanabi, calm down."

"Yeah, Tama! Relax."

When Tama-chan refused to back down, Hinami and Mimimi intervened to stop her.

"...But..."

She bit her lip in frustration and glared at the class queen. But Konno didn't even glance in her direction; she just kept chatting with her group and having a great time.

I watched it happen over and over during the past few days.

Another time, all of Tama-chan's spare pencil leads were broken. When she discovered them, she walked deliberately over to Konno.

"Konno! Keep your hands off my stuff!"

"...What? Ugh, what are you talking about?" she answered, looking bored.

"Stop playing innocent!"

"Would you stop getting so close to me? I don't want to get hurt. You shouldn't hit people, y'know?"

"...Ugh! You are so infuriating!"

Tama-chan kept fighting, refusing to back down in the least, but Erika Konno hardly listened. She just kept on accusing Tama-chan of "violence," as if she were in the right.

"Come on, Tama! It's lunchtime!"

"If we don't hurry someone will take the window seats! C'mon, Hanabi!"

Once again, Hinami and Mimimi tried to defuse the situation.

And so on and so forth for the next few days.

Little by little, something seemed to be falling away.

I'm sure that before all this started, Tama-chan was already the type of person who followed through on her decisions with no thought for the mood. That's what attracted Hinami and Mimimi to her and made them want to protect her. She had her own unique strength, an important core at the very center of her heart.

But that's exactly what made her vulnerable.

There was the time she'd almost gotten into a fight with Nakamura in home-ec class. And Hinami told me she actually *had* gotten into a fight with him in the past, and I doubt that was the only time something like that happened. Tama-chan had said herself that she had a hard time fitting in with the group, and that's why she was so grateful to Mimimi. That core was her strength, but it was also a double-edged sword.

With each little aggression from Erika Konno, and each act of resistance from Tama-chan, it was happening more and more…

"Hanabi-chan really seems to be having a rough time…"

"Yeah…first Hirabayashi-san, then Hanabi-chan. She'll go after anybody."

"Exactly. You can't get away from it as long as Konno-san's around."

"Man, I wish we could hurry up and change classes."

"Natsubayashi's amazing, huh? I bet Konno never guessed she'd get that much blowback. I could never do it myself."

"Seriously. You'd never guess from her looks, but she has guts."

"Agreed. Now it's basically a fight, huh?"

"Uh-huh. And I hope Natsubayashi wins."

"Like, okay… Yeah, Konno-san's awful, but I've gotta say, Natsubayashi-san is kiiiinda overreacting. Not that she's done anything wrong, of course!"

"Yeah, I think so, too. If she could just be a little more careful, I'd totally take her side…"

"…I wish she would think about all of us who have to watch their little drama every day."

"Yeah, exactly!"

"There she goes again."

"Uh-huh. God, can't she just stop? She's blowing this way out of proportion."

"It's not like Konno's gonna change or anything."

"Yeah, she's just gonna make it worse."

"How many times has this already happened today? Seriously."

"Don't ask me. Why does Natsubayashi have to get so mad?"

"I know Konno's being a bitch, but doesn't she know all this arguing just ruins class for the rest of us?"

"Don't you think she's kind of asking for it?"

"She never pays attention to how other people feel."

"Okay, she is taking this way too far."

The mood in class was getting worse and worse.

Another week passed.

* * *

We were in the classroom before the teacher arrived.

"Isn't it cute? I bought it the other day. Do you want one, too?"

Mimimi was talking to Tama-chan. In one sense, this was completely normal. They weren't talking about anything important.

"Are you kidding? It's not cute at all. I bet Tomozaki's gonna say it's ugly again."

"Aww, that's mean! Just look at it for a while; it'll grow on you."

"I don't believe you!"

"I'm serious!"

The only difference was the volume of their voices. Up till now, they'd been yakking away and messing around so loudly that they'd affected the mood of the whole class. Now they were talking so quietly that no one else could hear them. It was like they were afraid their voices would stray beyond the territory allotted to Tama-chan. You could hardly believe that not long ago, Mimimi would have been making loud jokes while Tama-chan shouted for her to cut it out.

There was a simple explanation for this change.

* * *

The mood of the class no longer allowed Tama-chan to speak in a loud voice.

Not Tama-chan herself, and not any group conversation that included her. In fact, any loud voices in class were undesirable.

The mood had deteriorated to a point where you could feel that rule.

Every minute or two, someone would shoot a curious, slightly hostile glance toward an imaginary circle around Mimimi and Tama-chan. No one was going to directly exclude her, but there was a general sense that people were annoyed, and they avoided walking near her. On the other hand, it didn't reach a more severe level of bullying, where their actions would extend to other members of her group. Hinami had just barely managed to stop the mood of the class from becoming explosive.

"Erika is really going too far lately, isn't she…?"

Hinami's group had gathered during break, and she was manipulating the mood. Since it was one of the top groups in the class hierarchy, midlevel girls would gather around hoping to one day become a member. At the moment, she was busy telling them how awful Konno's behavior was.

"Hanabi is trying hard to act strong, but underneath, she's really hurt…"

She was using every weapon she had to appeal to their emotions and gain their empathy. She even drew on their negative feelings toward Erika Konno. These easily influenced, midlevel girls didn't have strong opinions of their own, so she was doing everything she could to win them over. She was careful not to repeat herself too much during the breaks so she wasn't pushy, but she made sure that what she did say had force.

And so by using her own popularity, she managed to keep the class mood under control.

Mimimi was in charge of caring for Tama-chan while Hinami cooled down the general atmosphere. Between the two of them, they managed to hold off anything irreversible.

*** * ***

That day, my morning meeting with Hinami began with a long silence on her part.

"Tama-chan… She's in real trouble, isn't she?"

"Yeah…"

Hinami chewed her lip anxiously, her eyes restless. I didn't hear her usual strength in her voice. In fact, she sounded almost scared. To me, she was behaving like an ordinary girl without much confidence, which was about as much weakness as you could glean from the flawless gamer Aoi Hinami.

"…What's wrong?"

Her only reply was a quiet "mm" before she fell silent again.

So I talked instead.

"If this keeps up…she'll get more and more isolated, won't she? Right now it's not so bad because you and Mimimi are protecting her, but…"

The situation was worse than I'd thought. Every time Erika Konno and Tama-chan argued, Hinami and Mimimi skillfully intervened to stop them. Mimimi stayed by Tama-chan's side as much as possible to support her emotionally, so Tama-chan wasn't upset all the time. I saw her smiling several times per day. Meanwhile, Hinami was engaging in daily battle with the mood, using every means possible to keep things calm and save what she could of Tama-chan's image.

Now that she was out in full force, the power of Aoi Hinami was truly stunning. The control she had over the mood would have been unimaginable for most people. But nevertheless—nothing was improving.

Because Tama-chan refused to stop resisting and arguing with Konno over and over, the class's resentment was building up daily. At some point, those bad feelings would start to take root deep down, like stains on a teacup that couldn't be washed away.

On top of that, each argument was affecting people more and more just because it was happening again and again and again. Their frustration was gradually ballooning.

All the same, Hinami kept fighting to soften, blur, or completely cover up the negativity left behind by every argument. It was truly a feat that only Aoi Hinami was capable of. And she was up against Tama-chan.

If Hinami hadn't been there, her position in class probably would have already fallen beyond recovery. She might not have even been able to have those normal, quiet conversations with Mimimi anymore.

"Yeah…this can't keep happening. I've gotta do something…"

"Do something…?"

Something about that made me uneasy. Specifically, the fact that Hinami was choosing to handle the problem this way.

"Um…Hinami?"

"…What?"

I mean, that wasn't usually how she acted. I didn't think her approach was wrong or that it shouldn't be done. On the contrary, I thought it was a legitimate possibility.

But it simply felt off. It wasn't a Hinami-like approach.

I chose my words carefully so she wouldn't misunderstand me.

"Um, right now, I think our priority is to help Tama-chan… That's more important than anything else."

"…So…what?"

Hinami looked me in the eye with her own, indecipherable gaze. I couldn't make out the emotion in her eyes, but whatever it was, it was dark. I tried to put the inconsistency I'd noticed into words.

"Well, if we want to do that, we could, like, ask her to stop going after Erika Konno, or—"

"No. We can't."

Her eyes felt like they'd pull me in body and soul, and her voice was full of powerful determination as she flatly rejected my suggestion.

"…Why not?" I asked, frightened by her appearance in a different way than usual. Although her expression was uncharacteristically neutral, her eyes were sharp as knives.

"Hanabi isn't in the wrong. I told you before, didn't I? She just speaks her mind. Her heart and her words are completely unvarnished. That's why we can't."

Hinami's words were clumsier than usual and not entirely convincing in their logic. I'd never seen her like this before, and I wasn't sure if I should keep pushing the subject. At any rate, she seemed so unstable right now that I thought I'd better not contradict anything she said.

"But...why not?" I mumbled.

When she answered, she sounded like she wasn't talking to me. "Hanabi is in the right. What's wrong is the situation around her. She doesn't need to change."

"You mean..."

I realized something. Her argument itself made sense. If there was a right side and a wrong side, then the wrong side should change. That was a legitimate opinion. After all, that's my own basic approach to life.

Nevertheless, it felt strange coming from her. This was the polar opposite of everything Hinami had ever said up till now.

"If Hanabi doesn't manage to solve the problem without changing who she is...then it's meaningless."

Still, for some reason, she sounded very insistent on this point.

"Hinami..."

This wasn't how she usually handled things.

It doesn't matter how confident you are that you're right; if you can't get the rest of the world to agree, then being right is pointless. That's why you have to get people to accept what you believe, even if it means climbing into your opponent's ring and wearing a mask in the process.

In other words, if the situation is wrong, you adapt yourself to it anyway, and you fight.

That was her creed. It was what had gotten her through life so far. In which case, it made sense for Tama-chan to change and resolve the current problem.

Normally, Hinami would reach that conclusion. So why was she saying the opposite thing now?

Tama-chan didn't need to change because the situation was wrong, she'd said. And that wasn't all. When we weren't sure whether to help Nakamura or Hirabayashi-san, she'd even declared there was no need to help because they didn't follow her own approach to life. The gap between her attitude then and now was inconsistent, even contradictory.

"It's fine. I'll change everyone's minds."

Hinami wasn't looking at me. Yes, the will and determination on her face were undeniably powerful. But it wasn't like Izumi's supple strength. I felt like her determination was a little bit twisted, as if it was glued in place and wouldn't bend an inch.

* * *

One day, Mimimi skipped track practice.

That same day, Tama-chan and the volleyball team had no practice because of something that happened with the courts in the gym. Mimimi didn't want her to have to go home alone, so she decided to go with her and invited me to come with them.

And that's how the three of us ended up walking to the station together.

The two girls were being their usual selves.

"Hey, Tama! You've got some crumbs on you! Looks like some of that pie you ate earlier!"

"Oh, really?"

"Wait a sec… Okay, got it. Yum!"

"Ugh! Why'd you eat that?!"

They seemed as close as ever and as crazy as ever, and since they weren't in school, they were talking in their usual loud voices. It made me realize how much they'd been holding back in class.

"Mimimi, you're leaving Tama-chan behind."

"What?! Am I, Tama?! No way, right?"

"You totally are! I can't keep up with you!"

"Shot down!"

"…Ha-ha-ha. You walk too fast, especially lately."

"Not you, too, Tomozaki!"

I tried hard to play along and act normal, using all my skills to make sure that short window was fun, at least.

"See you later, Tama!"

"Yeah, see you tomorrow."

"Bye!"

When we got to the station, Mimimi and I said good-bye to Tama-chan, who was going in the opposite direction. She waved at us and smiled as she got onto her train, while Mimimi waved dramatically with her whole arm. Tama-chan smiled awkwardly back.

The door closed, and the train pulled away from the platform.

Mimimi kept waving with all her might until the train finally disappeared. She slowly lowered her arm, and the cheerful smile she'd been wearing fell away. I heard her sigh softly. She stood on the quiet platform, a lonely smile playing on her lips.

"...How did this happen?"

Her question was vague, but it seemed to contain all her emotions. I gazed out at the farm fields not far from the station.

"Bad luck and bad timing?"

"Luck and timing, huh?" Mimimi murmured listlessly.

I really thought that's what it was. Hinami had said the same thing. All the individual events had all lined up in the worst possible pattern and then slowly fallen, one after the next.

And now they had reached the final, giant domino that was about to slowly crush something very important.

If the main offender was Erika Konno, why had it all started in the first place? Why had it grown so out of proportion? The only answer I could think of was that a chain of small events had just...escalated.

"Yeah...I don't think it could have been prevented," I said, frustrated.

Mimimi kept scowling at the ground.

"Tama-chan hasn't done anything wrong, but everyone's treating her like a criminal. I hate watching this happen!!"

She clenched her fist and smashed it into her thigh. She was trembling, like all the frustration she felt had made its way into her arm.

"...I know."

Tama-chan really hadn't done anything wrong. Her only mistake was calling out Konno. That, and the fierce way she brushed off the embers of hostility falling all over her. Still, her reputation was slowly worsening.

The question of who was right and who was wrong had disappeared before anyone had even noticed, and now she was being treated like the criminal. Simply put, this was wrong.

Mimimi's arm flinched. When I looked up at her face, she opened and closed her mouth a few times before she finally spoke.

"Um, Tomozaki..."

"...What?"

She turned toward me and looked me in the eye, full of anxiety. Her lips were trembling slightly.

"Am I...doing a good job?"

"...Yeah."

"Am I keeping her going?" Uncertainty tinted her eyes. "When I'm with Tama, do I sound as happy as before?"

Her eyes were moist, clinging to me for reassurance.

"Do I still sound like I'm having fun when I laugh...?"

She asked me so earnestly; she wasn't even trying to hide her anxiety over whether she had been playing her part well in front of Tama-chan. These were her real feelings. And so I listened with equal earnestness and answered as seriously as I knew how.

"Yes...I think you've been doing great."

"Really? I didn't seem like I was trying too hard?"

"...Not at all."

"Okay..."

She sighed quietly, then suddenly looked up straight ahead, like she'd come to a decision.

"Tama-chan helped me when I was having a rough time...and I love her for it. I want to help her now, even if I can't do much."

"...Yeah, I can see that."

"But I'm not as good at this stuff as Aoi is, and I'm not as smart as you... All I can do is stand by her until she stops fighting with Erika."

"I don't think—"

Mimimi took a deep breath, like she was gathering all her energy.

"It's okay! I don't mind."

She still looked anxious, but now she was smiling slightly.

"It may not be much, but…if I can help her a little, then that's what I want to do," she said.

"…Huh."

"…Do you think I'm managing to distract her at least a bit?" Mimimi asked in an artificially cheerful voice. She clasped her hands behind her back, leaned forward, and peered up at me. I nodded as confidently as I could.

"Yeah. I definitely think you're helping her."

She stood up straight, pressed her lips together, and nodded slightly.

"Really? Okay, then… Okay."

She turned away from me and moved her hand up by her face—it looked like she was rubbing her eyes. Eventually, she put her hand down and spun back. Then she coughed, as if to clear the air. I felt like a little bit of her usual positive, forward-facing sparkle was back.

"Yeah…I have to stand by her!"

Still, I noticed her fists were shaking slightly.

* * *

The next day, as usual, Konno was harassing Tama-chan, and Tama-chan was digging in her heels.

"You messed with my pencil case again, didn't you?!"

"Come on, are you accusing me *again*?"

The rest of the class watched with annoyance. It was mild irritation, but Tama-chan was still the target. As usual, Hinami and Mimimi held Tama-chan back. I'd watched the scene a hundred times, but it still hurt just as much as before.

This time, I wasn't just watching.

I was observing and analyzing in order to find some way to help. After all, Tama-chan was in big trouble. I didn't want things to be this way. If I told myself I was too weak to deal with this and just looked the other way, nothing would improve. Hinami had said I was good at analyzing the situations I was handed. And I was nanashi, an even better *Atafami* player than she was. I should be able to do something that she couldn't. Or so I told myself for encouragement as I started to think about how this might finally end.

* * *

If I had to guess, the ending Mimimi wanted was one where Erika Konno burned herself out. By constantly standing by Tama-chan's side and taking care of her, Mimimi was buying time to prevent her from getting hurt too badly and letting Konno win. Meanwhile, she would wait for Konno to lose steam in her harassment campaign. If it stopped, that would be a good ending.

Or maybe she was hoping Tama-chan would stop rebelling. If that happened, then at least the tension her rebellion was causing would disappear, and her image among our classmates would improve. Konno's harassment might not stop, but the big picture would take a turn for the better. After that, all Mimimi had to do was keep up her emotional support for Tama-chan and wait for Konno to decide she was done. Without the rest of the class on her case, too, they should be able to hold up.

The problem with both of these approaches was that if Tama-chan was hurt so badly that Mimimi's care couldn't make up for it, the damage would be irreparable. That was a major issue.

On the other hand, my guess was that Hinami was aiming for two things. First, like Mimimi, she wanted Erika Konno to succumb. But unlike her, Hinami was tending to the whole class instead of to Tama-chan's mental state. She was buying time by cooling down the mood, and if Konno ran out of energy in the meantime, then that would be a good ending.

But I didn't think that was Hinami's favorite option.

Her real goal was more likely to send *the class mood flooding in the opposite direction.*

Currently, the mood was on the verge of laying the blame on Tama-chan. By forcefully flipping that mood on its head, she would make sure Konno took the fall. She would send the mood in an upstream deluge that would sweep Konno away, putting an end to the trouble by using the group and its mood to beat her into submission. She would take wrong-headed flow and put it back on course. I'm fairly sure that was the outcome she envisioned.

"I'll change everyone's minds."

I think that's what she meant by those words. In that case, the good ending would happen when she successfully reversed the class mood. If Tama-chan reached her breaking point before Hinami finished her work, that would be a bad ending. But to be honest, I couldn't help thinking it would be impossible, even with Hinami's power.

In other words, there were three possible ways for this problem to be resolved.

First, Erika Konno could give in to Tama-chan's resistance.

Second, Tama-chan could stop rebelling, and the mood could improve.

Third, the class mood could be forced to reverse course.

I think this was the range of endings Hinami and Mimimi were hoping for.

But what should I—what should nanashi—make of it all?

The answer was clear from the start.

A fourth ending.

* * *

After school that day, I went to the library. But I didn't go there to see Kikuchi-san. She didn't go to the library after school anyway.

I went there to wait for volleyball practice to end. While I waited, I didn't even pretend to read. I just sat and pulled together my thoughts.

I was thinking about what I wanted right now—about the fourth ending, the ultimate goal I was aiming for in this situation. The most important thing wasn't to prevent Tama-chan from changing, and it wasn't to fight with all my might on the enemy's terms. Both of those were means, not ends.

There was only one essential goal: to keep Tama-chan from getting hurt.

That was it. All I had to do was figure out the safest and most efficient strategy for achieving that goal and implement it. Nothing should take priority above that. I didn't need any pointless rules. I'd do whatever it took to reach the goal, and if any rules got in my way, I'd ignore them. I'd make my way forward, even if the path I took was dirty or "wrong." That was something that NO NAME couldn't do but nanashi could. And what tactic did this situation demand?

Retreat. I was sure of it.

Fleeing from combat. The *escape* command.
It was a common solution to problems in games.
Basically, there was one thing I wanted Tama-chan to do.

Until the storm blew over, I wanted her to stay home from school.

Such a backward approach might require her to bend her way of thinking a little. And the storm might never blow over. But it would still be far better than letting her suffer a wound she couldn't recover from.

People might call her pathetic, or a loser, or a coward, or uncool, but none of it mattered. None of that was important.

What mattered right now was making sure she wasn't hurt. That was all.

Plus, if Tama-chan and Konno stopped arguing, the resentment people held toward Tama-chan would stop building up. In the meantime, Hinami and Mimimi could gradually repair the class mood. Izumi might be able to find a way to soothe Konno's irritation toward Tama-chan. I'd do what I could, too, with my own weak skills. And chances were good the problem would be resolved.

That's why I thought retreat was the least risky, most realistic, and most likely to succeed option even now, as bad as it was.

This was the fourth ending I was aiming for.

It was after six PM. I left the library and headed for class. Tama-chan was standing by the window, watching track practice below. I'd talked with her here a bunch of times after the student council election between Hinami and Mimimi ended—about Mimimi, Hinami, and myself. I'd learned a lot of valuable things from her, so I wanted to have one more good conversation with her here.

"...Tama-chan."

She jumped a little, then turned toward me, almost frightened. Her face held a mixture of anger and fear, but when she saw it was me, that tension drained away.

Simply hearing her name was enough to make her assume the speaker was hostile—I couldn't let this keep happening.

"What's wrong, Tomozaki?"

She replied with the same tone and expression she'd used when we talked here before.

"Um, nothing's wrong, but..." I tried to smile as naturally as possible.

"What?"

"I just felt like talking a little."

"...Oh, really?" she said, sounding unconvinced. Still, she smiled faintly, relaxing a little. At least it wasn't a no.

"Yeah, about this whole mess with Erika Konno."

I jumped right into the topic. Her eyes widened in surprise for a second, then softened into amusement.

"You know, Aoi said something to me recently."

"Huh?"

That was quite a jump, and I wasn't sure how to respond.

"She told me she thought you and I were kinda similar."

"...Interesting."

I was slightly surprised. I remembered Hinami saying that to me, but she'd said it to Tama-chan, too?

Tama-chan kept looking me straight in the eye. "I didn't really know what she meant at the time, but I've kind of started to get it, back when we were talking while Minmi was running herself into the ground, and just now, as well." She smiled.

"Get what?"

She didn't look away as she answered. "We both say exactly what we're thinking."

"Oh…yeah."

I nodded. That was definitely true. Hinami had even said that was my only strength, and I could see Tama-chan had the same tendency.

"Anyway, what did you want to say about this whole mess?" she asked, as bluntly as I did a minute ago. That ability was pure Tama-chan—she could easily and directly state things that other people found hard to say or hear—and I guess I'm similar. With her, I didn't have to obsess over how to phrase what I wanted to say next. I could just say it.

"I was thinking you must be having a hard time with Konno attacking you and everyone else avoiding you. And if so, then maybe you should find a way to get away from it all for a while," I told her, without mincing words. Tama-chan's expression didn't really change. She kept looking straight at me, and she didn't seem uncomfortable.

"Um, yeah, it's not easy. But…"

"…Hmm?"

She gave me a big, strong smile. "But I'm fine."

There was strength in her smile. Call it fight, or conviction, or just assurance that she was right; it was a kind of confidence based on her own internal standards. I liked that smile. It reminded me of my own pride in myself as a gamer holding the controller, and as a character who didn't lie to himself.

"Because you believe in yourself?"

"Yeah."

She nodded simply. My words were very abstract, but for some reason, I felt like she understood them perfectly.

"I'm fine because I know I'm right."

I had the feeling I knew exactly what she meant, too, and I nodded firmly.

"…Gotcha."

"She's in the wrong, and I'm in the right. No matter what she does to me, I won't give in. I have my own way of doing things that I believe in, and I would hate changing that even more than I hate all the crap she's doing to me."

"...Definitely."

I could sympathize with that. Right now I was living life as a bottom-tier character without confidence in his own actions. But that was only because I still hadn't mastered the rules of the game I was playing. It wasn't because I had no faith in myself—in fact, back when I believed life was a shitty, garbage game, I was totally convinced I was right until Hinami showed me otherwise. And I was happy with that. Those were the values I devoted my life to, heart and soul. I had that sense of conviction, so I didn't need anyone else to back me up.

That's why I'd practiced so hard at *Atafami*, a game I believed was worth my time, and became the best player in Japan. I never hesitated. It was my lifestyle and my value system. Now that I'd decided life was a good game, I was basing my actions on that decision. That sense was the root of everything—what I believe is who I am. I sensed the same thing in Tama-chan.

"Then...I think it'll work out."

I decided then and there to forget about everything I'd been planning to suggest to her, because I understood what she was getting at. And because I truly believed, from the bottom of my heart, that her position deserved respect above anything else.

That was far more important than Erika Konno's daily attacks or the way everyone else was avoiding her. Changing herself on the basis of a value system that she didn't believe in was far worse. And that's why things were fine as they were. They *had* to be like this.

Tama-chan nodded confidently again.

"As long as I can be myself, I can put up with anything."

The simple power of the "self" supporting that statement filled me with admiration.

"So yeah. I'll be all right."

There was no hesitation or uncertainty in her eyes—just the integrity of a girl who was honest about how she felt. I looked her in the eye and nodded.

"Okay, then. Never mind."

I decided to have faith—and believe that what she was doing was right.

She was confident, and she was able to sacrifice everything else to that conviction. In this situation, succumbing to someone else's values would be far harder. And that was why she'd chosen not to let Erika Konno get away with anything.

After all, there was something ten times, even a hundred times more important than stopping Konno from kicking her desk or breaking her things, or stopping everyone else from avoiding her.

Believing in herself until the end.

"Well, I'm here for you," I said, meeting her eyes with a completely serious, honest expression. Maybe I was assuming, but I felt like those few words were enough to express what I meant. She smiled kindly, like she understood everything, and after a pause, she answered:

"But you know, Tomozaki..."

That kind expression was the same as the one from when she hugged Mimimi back then, but for some reason, I glimpsed a powerful resolution behind that kindness. She radiated a quiet but overwhelming determination, much greater than you would ever imagine from someone so small. It wiped out all my other thoughts as she continued:

"Everyone is so sad right now."

Behind her sympathetic eyes, her deep frustration, sadness, and anger were almost tangible. All I could do was keep listening silently.

"That's why I want to change."

The kindness of her decision was impossible to put into words. She had the ability to believe in herself completely; she'd just said she could put up with anything as long as she knew she was right. But she was willing to throw all that aside for the sake of something else. I was floored.

"While I was talking, I could tell I really am like you. I say what I think, and I'm bad at putting on an act. But—"

She took a step toward me. It was a small, Tama-chan-like step, but it was a step across an invisible line on the classroom floor.

"You've really changed lately. You've gotten good at reading other people and smiling and fitting in. We're so similar, but you've really challenged yourself. And you've managed to change. You've showed me it's possible."

Her eyes were serious and incredibly powerful, so much so that I could never look away. She nodded once.

"That's why..."

She jabbed a finger at my face, the same way she always did. The motion was so intense that it almost made me laugh, but at the same time, I felt like I was as close as I'd ever come to the fundamental, unchanging core of her heart. Slowly, she formed her hand into a fist.

"I want you to teach me how to fight."

Her eyes burned with a warrior's spirit. She believed in herself, but she didn't want to hurt the people she loved—

—and so she wanted to change, even though she was right. Behind those eyes was a quiet, flickering flame of determination.

Afterword

Hello again, Yuki Yaku here.

Somehow, we've already reached Volume 4 of this series. Now that I think about it, I realize the first volume went on sale last May. This volume will go on sale in June, which means a little over a year has passed since my debut.

I think the environment around me has changed over this time. For instance, my own lifestyle has changed. More people are working to make these books better, and I've been blessed with fans who support my work.

I'm quite certain these many changes are not just internal but have gradually altered my state of mind as well. Every day brings small, new realizations. But one day, I suddenly noticed that amid all these changes, one thing hasn't changed.

And that is the modest sexiness overflowing from the thighs that Fly-san draws.

This time, I'd like you to have a look at Yuzu's leg peeking out from her skirt, just beneath the ad strip wrapped around the cover of this volume. My guess is that when you remove that strip, your eyes will naturally gravitate to her sensual thigh.

But did you notice the significant contradiction within that thigh? The inconsistency right there before you? On one hand, your gaze goes straight to that thigh. On the other, the thigh itself is so slender.

Although the thigh is imbued with an all-consuming attractive power, it is not actually very thick. Nevertheless, the sexiness within it is distinctive, fresh, and magnetic.

The simplest way to emphasize one element of an illustration is to draw it larger than the others. However, Fly has not utilized that approach. Instead, they have taken special care in their manipulation of line and structure.

Observe the feminine curves, the line of the skirt clinging to the skin, and the way the knee hides the inner thigh. These small, realistic touches come together to erase all artificiality from the drawing. The viewer feels not as if they are being shown something, but as if they are simply looking at what is. Thus, the cover takes on a special depth.

And now on to the acknowledgments.

To my illustrator, Fly-san, thank you for contributing not only to the book but to the preorder bonuses despite your busy schedule. It's been a pleasure to see so many of your illustrations. I'm a big fan.

To Iwaasa-san, my editor, you had to work through Golden Week this time instead of the New Year's holiday. Scary that we're getting used to this, isn't it?

Finally, to all my readers, thanks to your support, this series has been turned into a manga. I look forward to bringing you more good news in the future. For now, please accept my sincerest gratitude. I hope you'll join me for the next volume.

Yuki Yaku